Sammy Keyes

and the Skeleton Man

So there we were, fighting through the bushes with
our flashlights bouncing around all over the place,
whispering and shhing our way towards the Bush House,
when out of nowhere this skeleton appears and comes
charging straight at us. All of a sudden I wasn't the
Monster from the Marsh any more. I was Sammy Keyes,
and my heart was looking for a way out of my body.

Read the first Sammy Keyes mystery...

Sammy Keyes
and the
Hotel Thief

And coming soon:

Sammy Keyes
and the
Sisters of Mercy

Sammy Keyes
and the
Runaway Elf

Sammy Keyes
and the Skeleton Man

Wendelin Van Draanen

■SCHOLASTIC

To Nancy Siscoe, a real treasure.

Special thanks to my husband, who continues
to show good humour even when I'm acting spooky;
to my family – both the in-laws and the outlaws –
for cheering me on; and to Mary Lou Prohaska and
Karen Macintosh, who know how to ring-and-run.
Thanks, too, to Bruce Miller at Phoenix Books, who
(not coincidentally) keeps his hair and sleeves quite tidy.

Scholastic Children's Books,
Commonwealth House, 1-19 New Oxford Street,
London, WC1A 1NU, UK
a division of Scholastic Ltd
London ~ New York ~ Toronto ~ Sydney ~ Auckland
Mexico City ~ New Delhi ~ Hong Kong

First published in the US by
Alfred A. Knopf, Inc., 1998

This edition published by Scholastic Ltd, 2003

Printed and bound by Cox and Wyman Ltd, Reading, Berks

10 9 8 7 6 5 4 3 2 1

Prologue

It's not like I was trying to get myself into trouble.

I was just out trick-or-treating like the rest of the kids in town. But then I got the bright idea that we should go up to the Bush House. I mean, it was Halloween, and banging on the Bush House door is kind of a tradition in Santa Martina. At least it's something everyone *else* always brags about doing, and I guess I thought it was time I tried it too.

We weren't expecting candy. We weren't even expecting anyone to answer the door. We were just expecting to scare ourselves half to death and then run away. Far away.

Trouble is, the door *did* open, and after what I saw inside, there was no way I could just turn around and run.

1

You may think I'm too old to go out trick-or-treating. Grams does. She thinks that after the fourth grade you're too old. Period. And seeing how I'm in the seventh grade, well, according to Grams I'm *way* too old.

And usually I pay attention to what my grams says. Partly that's because I *have* to since I'm staying with her while my mom's run off to Hollywood to become a movie star, but mostly it's because I've figured out the hard way that she's usually right about things. What she's definitely *not* right about, though, is the cut-off for trick-or-treating. I don't know exactly when it is, but I do know it's sometime *after* the seventh grade. Period.

Now Grams couldn't exactly make me stay home and pass out candy. Kids aren't even allowed in the Senior Highrise, so how can you pass out candy to them? She couldn't let me transform into the Monster from the Marsh in her apartment, either – not with Mrs Graybill waiting for me to slip up and give away the fact that I really *do* live with Grams. And since I didn't want to haul a bunch of green hair and warts and stuff clear across town to

3

Marissa's, when Dot invited us to get ready over at *her* house, I jumped up and said, "Great!"

Dot's new at school, and Marissa and I don't know her all that well, but I already like her. She's kind of quiet and blinks a lot, and always brings root beer in her lunch. Her name's really Margaret – or Maggie – but everyone calls her Dot because she's got a beauty mark right in the middle of her cheek. This is no mole. It's not lumpy or bumpy or poking out hair. It's just this round black circle on her face that looks like it's been coloured in with a fountain pen. A dot. And when you first meet Dot, you don't really notice that she's got big brown eyes and teeth that kind of crisscross in front – you just come away wondering if that's a *permanent* dot on her face, or if she was leaning on the wrong end of a marking pen.

Anyhow, I was stuffing everything I needed to transform into the Monster from the Marsh into a sack when Grams says, "Are you planning to go over *already*?" like Halloween is something you don't want to arrive too early for.

I just nod. "Could you check the hall for me?"

She rummages through my bag a little and says, "I want you to wear a jacket."

I look at her like she's crazy. "A jacket? But Grams . . . it's Halloween!"

Her hands pop on to her hips. "Young lady,

4

you're taking a jacket. It may not be that cold now, but in another hour it will be."

I roll my eyes and mumble, "Marsh Monsters don't wear jackets," but I go into her room and dig my jacket out of her bottom drawer because I know – there's no way she's going to let me out the door without it.

She gives me a little smile and says, "You've got your flashlight?"

"Yes, Grams!"

"Well then, it looks like you're set. Be home by nine, OK?"

I give her my best "pretty please?" look. "Nine-thirty?"

She sighs. "Not one minute after. It's a school night, Samantha."

I give her a kiss on the cheek and say, "I know, Grams, I know. Now could you check the hallway for me? Please?"

She opens the door a bit to see if Mrs Graybill's got her beak in the hallway waiting for me. She signals me that the coast is clear, so off I go with my sack of Marsh Monster paraphernalia, down the fire escape, out to Broadway, past the Santa Martina Town Centre Mall, and over to Tyler Avenue.

Dot lives in a skinny two-storey house on Tyler, right smack-dab in the middle of a bunch of other skinny two-storey houses, only Dot's house had about ten jack-o'-lanterns on the porch.

Seeing all those jack-o'-lanterns got me pretty excited about turning into the Monster from the Marsh. Halloween's the best. You don't have to worry about not having enough money to buy presents or wonder if someone's going to remember to get *you* something. You don't have to worry about cooking or cleaning or going to church – you just get dressed up and go out with your friends and have fun.

I raced up the steps, rang the doorbell, and kind of bounced up and down in my high-tops, waiting for someone to invite me in. And when Dot's dad answered the door, well, I didn't notice right away that he had big brown eyes and teeth that kind of crisscross in front. All I noticed was that right smack-dab in the middle of his cheek was a black spot, just like Dot's.

I stood there like an idiot for a minute, staring at Dot's dad's dot, and finally I say, "Hi, Mr DeVries? I'm Sammy . . . Dot's friend? Is she home?"

He smiles real big, which kind of pushes his dot up towards his eye. "So nice to meet you, Sammy. Come right in."

So in I go, into the Land of Blue. The carpet's blue, from about a metre down the walls are blue, and above that there's blue-and-white checkered wallpaper with ceramic plates mounted on it. *Dozens* of ceramic plates with blue windmills and cows and kids in wooden shoes.

Mr DeVries bends out of the way as a little girl dressed up as Snow White goes charging behind him. She's clicking a toy gun around in the air, shouting, "Pughh, pughh!" and a second later Mr DeVries has to jump out of the way again as another little girl in a cowboy hat and boots goes chasing after Snow White, waving a magic wand in the air. She's shouting, "Take this back! I want my gun! Give it back, or I'll turn you into a newt!"

The first girl calls, "Snow White doesn't carry a magic wand!" and a second later she comes whipping back around the corner, whispering, "What's a newt, Daddy?"

"A salamander, honey. Now, don't you think—"

Snow White dodges the Cowboy, crying, "Eee-haw!"

Mr DeVries gives me a little shrug and then calls up the stairs, "Margaret! Margaret, you've got a visitor!"

Dot comes racing down these skinny little stairs with her face looking like it's been half dunked in a bucket of yellow paint. She blinks a bunch, then says, "Hi, Sammy! Come on up!"

Dot's got a big family. She has two older

7

brothers and two younger sisters, and because they live in this skinny little house, all the girls sleep in one skinny little room and the boys sleep in another.

When you go into the girls' room, you move from the Land of Blue to the Land of Yellow. There's a yellow bedspread and a little yellow end table; one whole wall is painted yellow, and there's even a yellow chest of drawers. And standing there in the middle of all that *yellow* is Dot, painting herself to match the furniture.

I sit down on the edge of her bed and say, "So what are you going to be?"

She gives me a great big yellow smile. "A bee! Wait till you see my costume. It's gonna be great!"

She goes back to smearing yellow paint on her face, and I'm thinking *A bee?* when she says, "How about you?"

I start digging though my bag and say, "The Monster from the Marsh."

She looks at me in the mirror. "The Monster from the *Marsh*? What's that?"

All of a sudden I feel pretty stupid. Here she is, taking a bath in yellow paint, trying real hard to look like an enormous bee, and all I'm planning to do is rat my hair up, spray myself green, and call myself a Marsh Monster. Like there's such a thing.

I look at her in the mirror and kind of shrug. "It's just something I made up. You'll see."

She turns to face me. "Is that what you're going to be for Heather's party tomorrow night?"

Now the last thing I want to do is spend my favourite night of the year talking about Heather Acosta and her stupid party. I think Heather's throwing a party partly so she can do what she did last week: come up to me and say, "In case you hear about the party, it's true; everyone's invited – everyone but *you*." Can you believe it? That's exactly what she said. Then she wobbled her snobby red head, gave me her best nah-ne-nah look, and walked away. I tell you, having Heather Acosta in your life is like having a slice of onion on your peanut butter sandwich.

Anyhow, Dot's looking at me, waiting for me to tell her what I'm going to be for Heather's stupid party, so I kind of shrug and say, "Nah . . . I'm not going."

Dot's eyes pop wide open. "You're *not*? Why not? Everybody's going!"

Just then the doorbell rings. Then we hear, "Margaret! More company!"

Dot puts down her paint and jumps up. "That must be Marissa!" She races off saying, "This is so much fun!"

I was glad Marissa had shown up. We've been best friends since the third grade, and she doesn't have to ask what I'm going to be for Halloween. She knows that I'm going to be the Marsh Monster. That or the Ice Monster, if I happen to get white paint instead of green.

Anyway, Marissa comes in and gives me a great big smile. She says, "Sammy!" and puts down these two big shopping bags. "Ready to get ready?"

I nod. "What'cha gonna be?"

She dumps out one of the bags. "A mummy!"

Dot and I look at the rolls of toilet paper tumbling out of the bag and start cracking up. Dot says, "A *mummy*?"

Marissa pulls a white leotard and tights out of the other bag. "Yeah! And you guys are going to have to help me get dressed. C'mon!"

Just then the door bangs open, and Snow White comes whipping into the room. She slides under one of the beds, then yanks her skirt into the shadows just as the Cowboy charges in. The Cowboy stands in the middle of the room holding the magic wand out like she's warding off demons. "Where's Beppie?"

Dot barely nods her head towards the bed, but that's all the Cowboy needs. She calls "Eee-haw!"

and pounces. And as they're tearing each other up under the bed, I ask Dot, "Shouldn't you do something about that?"

Dot shrugs. "They'll work it out. They always do."

After a few more squeaks and squawks and *pughh, pughhs*, the Cowboy emerges with a gun in her hand and a smile on her face. She looks at Dot and says, "There's a newt under your bed," then disappears.

Dot looks at me. "What's a newt?"

Snow White comes out with a pout. "A salamander." She throws the magic wand on the ground, says, "I hate being a newt," and stomps out of the room.

Marissa and I shake our heads, then go back to getting ready. Marissa gets into her tights and leotard, and we wrap her up like a caterpillar in a cocoon, laughing and telling her what a great idea it is to be a mummy – if she trips and falls or bumps into something it won't even hurt because, really, she's got about fifteen centimetres of padding all the way around her.

When we're all done, she walks over to Dot's bed like the Abominable Snowman and stands there for a minute before she says, "I can't sit down!"

Dot and I start laughing all over again, but there's not much we can do about it. She has to just stand there while Dot and I hurry up and get ready.

So I'm hanging upside down, ratting and spraying my hair like crazy when Marissa says through the slit for her mouth, "Hey! I almost forgot! I brought you something." She goes over to her bag and pulls out this huge olive green sweater that's made out of long twisty strands that look like thick hair.

My eyes bug out. "Wow! Where did you *get* that?"

She smiles through all that toilet paper. "Yolanda's closet, of course."

"Your *mother* bought that?" I ask, thinking there's no way Mrs McKenze would be caught dead in a sweater that was obviously meant to be worn by a Marsh Monster.

Marissa says, "Yup, and I figure since I've never seen her wear it, she's not going to miss it." She hands it to me. "It's kinda heavy."

She wasn't kidding about that. I pop it on over my turtleneck, and all of a sudden I feel like I'm at the dentist, wrapped up in a lead apron, waiting for x-rays.

I move around a bit, swaying from side to side, getting used to this hairy sweater brushing against my thighs. Then I let out a few *Rrrrs* and *Arghs*, and pretty soon I'm *feeling* like the Marsh Monster. I go back to putting on warts and spraying hair, and when I'm all done I spread out my arms and say, "Hey! What'cha think?"

12

Marissa says, "That's great!" but Dot takes one look at me, pops on her antenna headband, and says, "Your shoes don't go."

I look down at my high-tops and then back at Dot. "They don't?"

She laughs. "They're white!"

Well, they weren't exactly white. They were too old to be white. But she was right. They sure weren't green.

Marissa shrugs and says, "So spray 'em."

I have to think about this a minute. Painting my hair and face and *hands* green, that's one thing. But my high-tops? I pick up the paint and read the label. It says WASH OFF WITH WARM SUDSY WATER, so I figure OK, what the heck, I'll spray my high-tops green.

Dot says, "I'm dying of thirst. Anyone else want a root beer?"

Marissa says she does, but I just shake my head and get to work painting my shoes. So Dot runs off, and a minute later she and Marissa are sipping root beers, watching me work. And when my shoes are finally all green and dry enough to wear, I lace them up and say, "Is that better?"

Dot says, "Much!" and Marissa nods. "That's the best Marsh Monster ever."

Dot gives herself one last look in the mirror,

adjusting the wings that are strapped on like a backpack. "So where are we going to go?"

Marissa puts down her root beer. "Why don't we start here and go out towards Broadway?"

Dot says, "I thought maybe we'd go the other way. You know, up the hill? They probably have great decorations and candy and stuff up there."

Marissa and I laugh because we tried that once. We went all around Marissa's neighbourhood and came home with practically nothing. Big houses are rotten for trick-or-treating. You have to run like crazy to get from one house to the next, half the houses have their lights off, and if they *do* have their porch light on, half the time the people don't even know it's Halloween. They answer the door and just kind of stare at you, and you can see them thinking, *Are these kids dressed up for a reason? Is it Halloween? No, it can't be. . .* Then off they go to dig up some marshmallows or nuts that they've got buried in a cupboard somewhere, and the minute you turn around, *click*, they've doused the porch light.

Anyhow, we agreed that we'd start off in Dot's neighbourhood and work our way over towards the mall. And it might have been just a regular Halloween night for the Bee, the Mummy and the Monster from the Marsh, if I hadn't got the bright

14

idea to take Dot somewhere she'd never been before. A place you wouldn't dare go except on Halloween. A place even adults don't like to talk about.

A place all the kids in town call ... the Bush House.

The Bush House isn't scary because it has a big pointy roof and broken shutters. You see that kind of stuff all the time. And it's not scary because it's haunted – it's not. No, the Bush House is scary because of the *bushes*. They're dry and gnarly, and they've got so big that they've kind of swallowed up the house.

The bushes start clear out by the street and go up about three metres in the air. Then they kind of arch over the sidewalk and connect with the ones that are growing in the yard. You can be walking down the sidewalk in the middle of the day with the sun beaming away up in the sky, and if you're crazy enough to walk through that tunnel of bushes instead of crossing over to the other side of the street, well, the sun disappears. And there you are in the dark with your heart thumping and your knees bumping because you just know that the Bush Man's going to jump out and kill you.

No one had ever actually seen the Bush Man. No one that I believed, anyway. Grams had told me that the stories about him were exaggerated – that he was probably just a lonesome man lost in his own world, but I never quite believed her, either. No, there's something very strange about a man who locks himself up in a house like that, and the best thing to do is stay away from him and his bushes.

The Marsh Monster didn't happen to agree. And it's the Marsh Monster who dragged the Bee and the Mummy down Orange Street, through the tunnel, and on to the Bush House walkway. And it's the Marsh Monster who said, "C'mon! It'll be fun!"

So there we were, fighting through the bushes with our flashlights bouncing around all over the place, whispering and *shh*ing our way towards the Bush House, when out of nowhere this *skeleton* appears and comes charging straight at us. All of a sudden I wasn't the Monster from the Marsh any more. I was Sammy Keyes, and my heart was looking for a way out of my body.

Marissa screamed, but it must have scared the buzz right out of the Bee, because one minute Dot's up and the next minute she's on her little stinger in the middle of the walkway. And she's crawling backwards, trying to get away from the skeleton, when she steps on one of her wings and can't move.

Then we hear, "Out of the way, out of the *way*!" and that's when I realize that the skeleton's not a skeleton at all, but a trick-or-treater in one of those glow-in-the-dark skeleton suits. And he's sure had a busy night, because his green-and-white striped pillowcase is just *loaded* with candy. He swings it right over Dot's head and kind of dances around her, then disappears down the walkway.

For a minute, the three of us stare at where he used to be. Then I help Dot up and say, "And Grams thinks *I'm* too old to go out trick-or-treating."

Dot lets out a nervous little laugh, but you can tell – she wants *out* of there. I look over at Marissa, and, sure enough, she's doing the McKenze dance. She's got her toes pointed at each other, and she's squirming around with her knees together, biting on a fingernail, looking scared to death. She whispers, "I have to go."

I grab her by the arm. "Hey, don't be spooked – it was only a trick-or-treater. C'mon . . . the door's right there. We'll just knock and run, OK?"

"No, Sammy, I have to go!"

"Look, Marissa, we're never going to live it down if people find out we made it halfway up the walkway and—"

"Sammy . . . I have to *go*!"

I stare at her. "To the *bathroom*?"

She nods. "I shouldn't have had that root beer."

I look around and say, "Just go in the bushes."

Her eyes practically pop through toilet paper. "In the *bushes*? No way! Besides, I *can't*. I'm all wrapped up and I've got on tights and a leotard. I'm going to have to take off everything to go!"

I can't help it – I start laughing. I mean, there she is, buried in a mountain of toilet paper with no way to use it. Before you know it, Dot's laughing too, and Marissa says, "Stop it! It's not funny!" and then *she* starts laughing.

Finally I say, "Look, I'm just going to go up and knock on the door, and then we can go back to Dot's and you can go to the bathroom, OK?"

Marissa stops laughing. "You're going by *yourself*?"

I say, "Sure," because right then I wasn't feeling too spooked. So we're surrounded by a few out-of-control bushes – so what?

I run the rest of the way up the walkway and pound on the Bush House door, *wham! wham! wham!* like a jackhammer in church.

Then the door opens.

All by itself.

I should've run, but for some reason I just stood there, staring. I'd never even thought about what the *inside* of the house was like. But there I was, all by myself, standing in the pitch black on the porch, staring inside the Bush House. And inside would've been just as black as outside if it hadn't been for

19

this *fire* that was burning about halfway down the entry hall.

Now, this fire isn't in a fireplace. It's on the *floor* next to a skinny table, and it's burning up a bunch of newspapers. And even though it's dark inside, I can tell that in a few minutes the table's going to catch fire. I lean in a little bit and call, "Hello? Hello? Anybody home?" and of course no one answers.

I shine my flashlight inside, but the beam just gets swallowed up by the darkness. "Hello? Hey!" I shout. "Anybody home?"

Nobody answers, so I push the door open all the way, just in case the Bush Man's waiting behind it, ready to tie me up and roast me on his little open-pit barbecue.

Then I hear Marissa calling, "Sammy? Sammy! What's going on?"

I call back, "Come here! Hurry!" but I don't wait for her and Dot. I go charging into the house and start stomping on the fire with my high-tops. First I slap it with one foot, then I slap it with the other, and while I'm busy dancing on fire I notice that there's a candleholder in the middle of the flames.

Pretty soon the bottoms of my high-tops are melting and my feet are getting toasted, but is that fire giving up? Not a chance. I keep on jumping up and down wishing for a hose or a fire extinguisher, calling out at the top of my lungs, "Fire! Hey, fire!" When Marissa and Dot peek in the front door, I yell, "Get in here and help me!"

Dot tosses her candy sack down and comes flying in, but Marissa just stands in the doorway doing the McKenze dance. I yell, "Marissa, call the fire department!"

She says, "But..." and I can tell there's no way she's going to wander through the Bush House looking for a telephone or water or anything else.

Then it hits me. The Marsh Monster sweater. I yank it off and smother the flames with it. First I put it on one side of the fire, then I put it on the other. And it was pretty roasty there for a little while, but before you know it, the smoke's dying down and the fire's out.

I give Dot a high-five, and Marissa shuffles in and whispers, "What *happened*?"

"It looks like a candle started the fire."

Dot says, "How? There's nobody here."

We bounce our flashlights around for a minute, and then Marissa whispers, "Well then who lit the candle?"

We look at each other, our eyes getting wider and wider, and Marissa says, "Let's get *out* of here!"

21

I was planning to follow her right out the door, but something made me look around the corner at the end of the hall. And when my flashlight shone on him, I couldn't run. I could only scream.

Now you have to understand – I'm not the screaming kind. The only other time I've tried it, nothing came out. But this time it came out, all right – loud and clear. I went charging back around the corner, screaming my face off, and practically ploughed Dot over. And all my screaming made Marissa scream, and Marissa's screaming made *Dot* scream.

And the *reason* I'm screaming is because just around the corner, sitting in a chair with his head twisted around sideways, is Frankenstein. And I'm not talking a Frankenstein mask on a shirt stuffed full of hay, like you might see on someone's porch. I'm talking flesh-and-blood *alive*.

And even though my brain knows it can't really *be* Frankenstein, my *mouth* hasn't quite caught on – it just keeps right on screaming until I clamp a hand over it and shut it up.

Marissa clamps her own mouth shut, then cries, "What? What's back there?"

I know that if I tell her that Frankenstein's right around the corner with his head screwed on crooked, she'll freak out and start running, so I say, "Wait right here."

She grabs my arm. "Where are you *going*?"

I shake off her hand. "I've got to check something out, OK? I'll be right back."

My heart's going crazy inside my chest, and I can feel the rest of me getting shaky, but I make myself walk around the corner. I shine my flashlight on him, move a few steps closer, and then just stand there, looking.

Frank doesn't budge. He just sits there slouched sideways in the chair. Then I notice the ropes. There's one tying his hands together, and there's one wrapping his ankles to the legs of the chair. So I take a few steps closer, thinking that if he *is* alive, he sure isn't going to jump up and nab me.

Through the holes in the mask I can see hair – kinky grey and black hair. It's one of those heavy-duty masks that get all steamed up when you wear them; if you've ever put one on *sideways*, well, you know you can't breathe like that for very long.

So I reach forward, and I'm about to take off the mask when somebody screams.

I jump about three metres in the air, and as I'm coming down I look over and see Marissa. She says, "What *is* it?"

I put my heart back in my chest and say, "I think it's the Bush Man . . . and I think he's *dead*."

Marissa looks like she's about to run, but Dot comes inching in, whispering, "He's *dead*?"

Marissa follows her, kind of hiding behind Dot's wing, and while they're getting closer I reach out and pull Frankenstein's face off.

It's a man all right, and he *is* looking pretty dead. His head flops forward, and there's blood running from one side of his head down his cheek and into his beard. I put my hand under his nose to see if he's breathing, but I can't feel anything. Then I poke around his neck for a pulse. "He's *not* dead!"

Dot whispers, "He's *not*?"

I shake my head. "I can feel his heartbeat."

I look around for something to blot the blood off his face, and then I remember Marissa. I start yanking toilet paper off one arm, and Dot starts yanking it off the other. We blot a bit and figure out that the blood's coming from a gigantic bump above his ear.

As soon as we stop the bleeding, I check his breathing again. And I'm holding *my* breath, waiting for some air to come out of him when I notice that his chest is going up and down. Not very fast or far, but up and down. And I can't figure out why I can't feel any air, when all of a sudden he moves a little bit and we hear this wheezing sound.

I jumped. All of us did. I mean, this was the *Bush Man*. It had to be. And that wheezing sound wasn't coming from his mouth. I couldn't tell exactly *where* it was coming from, but it was pretty spooky-sounding, let me tell you. So there he is, wheezing and twitching, and what does he see when he opens his eyes?

A hairy green girl, a decomposing mummy, and a Godzilla bee.

And who screams?

We do.

And we're turning around to run, but just then the weirdest sound comes out of him — it's not a gurgle, and it's not a growl; it's something kind of in between.

Marissa yanks on my arm. "Come on! Sammy, come *on*!"

But something's telling me to stay put and listen. I say, "Shh! Shh!" and yank back.

Then we hear it again, that gurgling growl. Only this time it's louder, and this time I know — it's his *voice*.

And what he's saying is *"Help . . . me."*

Three

Marissa stops yanking and whispers, "What did he say?"

I whisper back, "I think he said, 'Help me.'" I grope along the wall for a light switch, but when I find it and flip it up, nothing happens. So I shine my flashlight on the man and call out, "Are you OK?"

He just holds out his wrists to me.

I move forward, but Marissa grabs me and whispers, "You're not going to un*tie* him, are you?"

"Marissa, he's hurt! Someone tied him up!"

"Maybe he was torturing them, and they just got away!"

Now from everything I'd ever heard about the Bush Man, this was not such a crazy thought. But there he was with his hands out, looking so helpless that I couldn't just leave him. I went over, got the knot out of the rope around his hands, and then ran back to Marissa and Dot and watched while he untied his legs.

When he's got the ropes off, I ask him, "Do you want me to call an ambulance?"

He touches the spot on his head where he's been

clobbered, and after a minute he shakes his head. Then he pulls a pencil and a little pad of paper out of his shirt pocket and scribbles something on it. He tosses it over to me, then goes back to feeling the bump on his head while we read: GO NEXT-DOOR TO 625 – NOT 629 – AND CALL THE POLICE. PLEASE. PS DID YOU SEE THE SKELETON MAN?

I think about this a second. "You don't have a phone?"

He shakes his head.

"Or electricity?"

He shakes his head again, and then that gurgling growl comes out of him. "Did ... you ... see ... him?"

"He practically ran us over on your walkway. Is he the one who knocked you out?"

He nods, so I say, "Did he rob you?"

He shrugs, then pats his hip pocket and nods again. Then all of a sudden he starts sniffing the air. "*Fire?*"

"Don't worry. It's out."

He crunches up his brow, then points to the pad. "Go ... call."

I nod, and I'm about to leave when I decide to ask, "You're the Bush Man, aren't you?"

He looks at me kind of funny, then shakes his head and shrugs like he's never heard of the Bush Man. "The ... name's ... LeBard."

Well, I'm not going to stand there and explain to him how *he* may think his name's LeBard, but everyone else in town calls him the Bush Man. I'm just going to go next-door and tell the police to come to the Bush House. They'll show up a lot faster than if I tell them 627 Orange Street.

So off I go, only Marissa grabs my arm and whispers, "You're not leaving us here *alone*, are you?"

I look around. "Do *you* want to go call?"

She nods real fast. "Yes!"

Trouble is, she takes Dot with her. So I'm left all alone in this dark house with the Bush Man, and part of me's scared, but part of me's curious. I mean, there are all these questions that I'm dying to ask, like *Why's the power off?* and *Why don't you have a phone?* and *Why do you have so many* bushes? But with him sitting there holding his head, well, they all seemed kind of stupid.

And I probably would've just stood there minding my own business while he rubbed his head, if there hadn't been this one question that kept popping up. Finally it just popped out. "What happened to your *voice*?"

He sits there looking at me a minute, then motions for the pad.

I toss it to him and pretty soon it comes flying back with TRACHEOTOMY/LARYNGECTOMY written on it.

I study the words, trying to figure out what they mean. Then I look at him and shake my head. "What's that?"

He pulls back his shirt collar and shows me his neck.

I tried not to stare but I couldn't help it, because right there at the base of his neck was a *hole*. It wasn't really that gross or anything – it was just a small hole. It's just not something you expect to see when you look at a person's neck.

I guess he got tired of me staring because after a minute he closes his collar and gurgles, "You . . . smoke?"

I just stand there like an idiot, shaking my head.

He nods. "Good."

I watch while he gets up and shuffles around the room lighting candles. And when the place is lit up a bit, I feel like I'm in some ancient museum of books. Old books. Books that look like they'd fall apart in your hands if you took them off the shelves. Books that are brown or dark green or black, with faded lettering on the side. *Scary* books.

I'm not talking one or two. I'm talking the whole room. Every centimetre of every wall. Well, there was a window that was covered up by a thick brown curtain, and there was a fireplace, but other than that every centimetre contained books.

He finishes lighting three candles at the far end of the room, then he walks over to a table next to the fireplace and stops. And he stands there for a long time, just staring. Finally he turns around, and even though no sound comes out of his mouth, you can tell – he's cussing.

Seeing the Bush Man with his wild hair and bumped-up head, holding a candle that's dripping wax while he's cussing away, well, I was ready to run. But right then there's a pounding on the front door and a voice calls in, "Hello? Mr LeBard? Police. . . Hello? These girls tell us you're in some sort of trouble. May we come in?"

The Bush Man takes a candle and shuffles off to the front door. And I'm standing there in the middle of all these flickering candles and books, thinking that the room looks like some kind of vampire heaven, when Marissa and Dot come racing into the room.

Marissa stands right in front of me, jumping up and down, whispering, "You'll never guess who's here!"

I say, "Oh *no*," because, looking at her, I know *exactly* who must have come to take the report. "You've got to be kidding."

She grins. "Nuh-uh, and he's in a *real* good mood."

I roll my eyes. "I don't *believe* this." Then I notice that Dot's still the Bee, but except for her tights and leotard Marissa is Marissa – not the Mummy. I ask, "Did you use the bushes?"

She laughs and says, "No, the people next-door let me use their bathroom."

Dot scratches under one of her antennae and whispers, "I don't get this. I don't get any of this. *Who's* in a real good mood? Are you talking about –" She pumps her skinny little arms like some champion bee wrestler.

I look at Marissa, and Marissa looks at Dot, and you can practically see a light bulb go on over Marissa's head. "Oh! No, not –" and then she pumps *her* arms and kind of squats, and then they both bust up.

Just then a police officer comes around the corner with the Bush Man, and right away I know what they're pumping and squatting about. The policeman's about a hundred and fifty-five centimetres and has more muscles than you'd need to bench-press a hippo.

He says to the Bush Man, "This is the room?" The Bush Man nods, so Muscles says, "Can we maybe get some *light* in here?"

Before I can stop myself, I say, "He doesn't have electricity, he doesn't have a phone, and he doesn't have a voice – well, not a regular one anyway. He's had a tracheotomy."

The police officer studies the Bush Man for a minute, then navigates all those muscles a little closer to me. "And you are. . .?"

Marissa jumps in. "She's my sister, remember? The one who found him?"

Dot looks at Marissa and then at me, and you can tell she's thinking, *Your* sister?

Then the reason Marissa has to lie about us being sisters comes walking around the corner. His Supreme Rudeness, Officer Borsch.

Officer Borsch isn't real fond of me. It's a long story, but let's just say that if he had the choice of winning the lottery or running me over with his squad car, I'd be sprawled out on the pavement.

And I do my best to steer clear of him, but there I was, standing in Vampire Heaven with my good buddy, Officer Borsch. I was hoping that he wouldn't recognize me, what with me being *green* and all, but he takes one look at me and says, "Oh, no. Not *you* again!"

I give him my best Marsh Monster smile. "Took the words right out of my mouth."

Dot's big brown eyes get even bigger. She

whispers, "Sammy!" just like Grams would've if she'd been there.

He ignores me and turns to Muscles. "There's nothin' outside – or if there is, you'll never find it in that mess." Then he says to the Bush Man, "You gonna be able to answer a few questions, or what?"

The Bush Man holds up a finger telling him to wait a minute, then goes over to a desk and starts to rummage through it.

When he comes back, he's carrying something that looks like a small electric razor. He sits down in his chair, then puts the thing up to his throat and out of him comes, "Please sit down." It wasn't a gurgle-growl like before. It was a mechanical kind of buzzing sound. And even though the words came out faster than they had earlier, it was still sort of hard to understand him.

Officer Borsch sits down, but Muscles eyes the other chair and keeps right on standing. So I sit down. Right next to Officer Borsch.

He sneers at me and says, "So I get the distinct headache of dealing with you again."

The Bush Man pushes the buzzer to his throat and says, "Don't you talk to her that way!" Then he looks straight at me and smiles. Not the kind of smile where you can see teeth and the person's eyes sparkle a little. No, more like he's trying to remember how to do something he hasn't done in a really long time. The corners of his mouth twitch a little, and his eyes look sad, just for a second – but I can tell, it's a smile.

I smile right back at him, because even though he's the Bush Man, I'm warming up to him.

He says, "What's your name? I believe I owe you a debt of gratitude."

He wasn't talking very fast, but there were a lot of *s* and *t* sounds missing, and understanding him was taking a little getting used to. "Sammy. Samantha Keyes."

He sticks out his hand. "I'm Chauncy LeBard. Call me Chauncy."

Well, what the Bush Man is doing with a name like *Chauncy* is a mystery to me, but just the same, I lean over and shake hands with him. "Hi, Chauncy."

Officer Borsch rolls his eyes. "Yeah, yeah – let's get on with it." He flips open his notebook and starts scribbling. And when he's done taking down Chauncy's name and address and stuff he says, "OK, Mr LeBard, the girls tell me they found you bound and unconscious in that chair. Tell me what happened."

Chauncy looks at him and buzzes, "When I answered the door, someone in a skeleton suit forced himself into the house. We struggled for a bit, but then he flung me against the wall. The last thing I remember is the candle flying out of my hand."

I ask him, "So you don't remember him tying you up?"

He shakes his head.

"What about the Frankenstein mask?"

He shrugs and shakes his head again. "A blindfold perhaps?"

Officer Borsch squints at him and says, "What do you mean by skeleton suit?"

He wasn't asking me, but I answered him anyway. "It's a suit that goes over your whole body – you know, like a Spiderman suit – only with bones that glow in the dark."

Officer Borsch gives me a thank-you-very-much-now-keep-your-stupid-mouth-shut smile and says to Chauncy, "How about height, weight, age? Anything else you can tell me about him?"

Chauncy thinks for a minute. "A hundred and seventy-five ... maybe a hundred and eighty centimetres. Eighty-five kilos ... maybe less. I have no idea about the age."

Borsch scribbles some notes, then says, "Did he say anything?"

"Not one word."

Marissa, Dot and I look at each other. "He did to us!"

Borsch-head can't exactly ignore us, but does he turn to me? No. He says to Dot, "What'd he say?"

Dot blinks a bit because she wasn't expecting to have to actually *talk* to Officer Borsch. She squeaks, "'Out of the way. . .'" then clears her throat and says louder, "He said, 'Out of the way.'"

Officer Borsch frowns and says, "From his voice, can you guess how old he is?"

"I don't know, sir. Maybe . . . eighteen?"

Officer Borsch just nods and says, "Figures," like he knew all along that it was some punk kid out causing trouble on Halloween.

But I'm looking at Marissa, and she's looking at me, and we're both pulling faces at each other because we think eighteen's way off base. But we don't want to say so, because if we jump up and say, "Eighteen? No way!" we'll embarrass Dot.

I guess Dot saw us because she says, "Don't you think so? Marissa? Sammy?"

Marissa shrugs. "I was thinking more like twenty-five."

I look at her and say, "Twenty-five? He was at least *thirty*-five."

Officer Borsch throws his hands up in the air. "Great. Girls, you've been a big help." Then he rolls his eyes like we've got beans for brains.

All this time Muscles has been standing there, pushing back the cuticles of his fingernails with a thumb, shifting from side to side like he's on a boat. He looks up from his swaying and says to Chauncy, "Why'd you answer the door? You don't look set up for trick-or-treaters."

Chauncy buzzes back at him, "You're right. Normally I don't answer. Mostly it's kids knocking and running, but this fellow was beating the door so hard and so long I thought it might be important."

Officer Borsch asks, "So what's missing? Your wallet? Anything else?"

Chauncy nods. "My wallet and a pair of pewter candlesticks... I don't know what else. I haven't had the opportunity to look around."

Officer Borsch asks, "Pewter? Isn't that some kind of *tin*?" as if Chauncy'd just reported a sack of garbage missing.

Chauncy shrugs. "Perhaps he thought they were silver."

Now Officer Borsch could've just nodded or said, *Could be*, or something like that, but what's he do? He gives Chauncy this stupid little smile and says, "Perhaps," like he's having crumpets and tea instead of taking a police report. And before Chauncy can quite absorb that one of Santa

Martina's finest is making fun of him, Officer Borsch stands up and says to Muscles, "Keith, I think we should take a look-see. Mr LeBard? Would you mind showing us around?"

Chauncy stands up, and while Muscles and Officer Borsch are whipping their flashlights off their belts, Chauncy's looking around like he's missing something. I realize that he doesn't have a flashlight, so I hand him mine and say, "Here you go."

There's that smile again, only this time the corners of his mouth go up a bit further and he gives me a little nod. And I'm about to tag along when Marissa grabs me by one arm and Dot grabs me by the other. They both start whispering a mile a minute, saying how the kids at school are not going to believe it when they hear how we spent Halloween *in* the Bush House and how we met the Bush Man and saved his life and how I shook the Bush Man's hand and stuff like that. And they're going on and on, but pretty soon I'm thinking about something else. I borrow Marissa's flashlight and go over to the table where Chauncy had been cussing.

I shine the light across it and, sure enough, there's dust everywhere. Everywhere except for these two spots where there's *no* dust. And I'm standing there thinking that it looks like someone drew two little stop signs right in the middle of the table, when Marissa comes up and says, "What are you doing?"

"I'm just looking." I move around the room, checking out the other candleholders, wondering why the Skeleton Man had picked the ones he'd picked and not any of the others.

Marissa and Dot follow me, asking, "What are you looking *for*?"

I tell them, "I don't really know," because I don't. I'm just looking.

I check out the rest of the candlesticks and then some pens and an old clock on the desk, and I'm just starting to run the light over a bookshelf when Officer Borsch and Muscles come back. They say their goodbyes and their if-you-need-anything-give-us-a-calls – like that's something Chauncy could do without a phone – and then Muscles calls, "C'mon, ladies. Party's over."

So we head out and when we're by the front door I get my flashlight back and say, "Bye, Chauncy!"

He mouths, *Bye*, only this time there's no smile. Not even a twitch.

The door closes and pretty soon we're flashing our lights down the walkway, surrounded by bushes again. When we get to the sidewalk, Officer Borsch says to me, "You keep out of this, you hear?"

I turn to him and smile. That's all, I just smile. And what does he do? He grabs my arm, gets right in my face, and sputters. He doesn't actually *say* anything – he just sputters. And his face is getting redder and redder, and he looks like he's about to start snorting and pawing the ground, but then he drops my arm and marches off. Just like that.

Muscles looks back and forth between us, but then chases after his partner. And while the three of us are standing there in the bush tunnel watching them go, I can't help thinking about Chauncy and the Skeleton Man and the Frankenstein mask. Why would someone rob the Bush Man, of all people? Who'd go through all that for a wallet and some candlesticks? What was the guy *thinking*?

And I don't have a lot to work with, but my brain's pretending that I do, so as I'm watching the squad car drive away I get this queasy feeling that I haven't seen the last of Officer Borsch.

And he hasn't seen the last of me.

Nine-thirty may not seem like much of a curfew to you, but you've got to understand – Grams always makes me come in by nine. So being late for a nine-thirty curfew is like crossing Broadway against the light – there's going to be a whole lot of honking, and no matter which way you turn you're in trouble.

I'd taken the fire escape, like I always do when I'm sneaking in for the night. But for once I wasn't really thinking that Mrs Graybill might catch me and get me kicked out of the building – in my mind, Mrs Graybill was already sound asleep. I was thinking that *Grams* might kick me out before I had a chance to explain things to her.

So I didn't even check to see if Mrs Graybill was still up. I just came barrelling down the hallway at a hundred and fifty kilometres an hour. And when I turned the corner and Mrs Graybill was standing in front of her apartment unlocking the door, well, the first thing I did was choke.

I don't know what *on*. I mean, I wasn't eating candy or anything. I just choked. So there I am, hacking away, wondering why on earth Mrs Graybill's wearing a dress that looks like a honeysuckle hurricane

41

instead of her old pink bathrobe, and my brain can't seem to come up with a decent lie about why I'm visiting my grandmother at ten o'clock at night with a sack of candy and a face full of green paint.

When I finally stop hacking, Mrs Graybill stands there with her fists on her hips. "Rita needs a sugar boost, I suppose?"

I manage to squeak, "Ha-ha! That's a good one!" Then I look at her like *she's* the one with a green face and warts and say, "I forgot my schoolbooks." I ring the bell and stare at her like I've got all the business in the world being where I am, and when Grams answers the door I say real loud, "Happy Halloween, Mrs Graybill!" and go inside.

Now Mrs Graybill's not going to just tuck herself in bed. She's going to hang up her honeysuckle hurricane, put on some thick socks and her old pink bathrobe, and wait. And if I don't come out of Grams' apartment in a few minutes, she's going to sick Mr Garnucci on Grams and me. Either that or she'll call the police again, and with my luck Officer Borsch will be the one taking the report.

So the minute I'm inside, I say, "Grams, I'm sorry I'm late, but there was an emergency," and then I tell her all about the Bush House and the fire and the mask, and about Chauncy and Officer Borsch.

The whole time I'm talking she doesn't say a word.

She just sits there staring at me, her eyes getting bigger and bigger, and when I'm all done, she takes a deep breath and says, "How do you get yourself into these things?" Then she says, "Chauncy? *LeBard?* That sounds like some kind of aristocratic English name." She turns and mumbles, "Certainly not a name I would've pictured for the *Bush* Man."

I shoot forward on the couch. "So you *do* know something about him!"

Grams smooths down her skirt. "All I know is gossip, and gossip is poison. Not something I want to spread around."

I felt like saying, *Tell me! Tell me what you know!* but I could tell by the way her chin was pushed forward that she wasn't about to spoon me any poison. I eyed her and said, "Did you know he'd had a tracheotomy?"

Her chin drops a little, and her head shakes back and forth.

"Did you know that he doesn't have any electricity?"

She pops her glasses off her nose and rubs them with the hem of her blouse. "No! All I know is that people say he went crazy after his mother died. There. Are you satisfied?" She pops her glasses back on her nose. "I've also heard he's dangerous – and obviously he's unstable. The fact that you went into

43

that house tonight. . ." She throws her hands up in the air and says, "Samantha, *why* did you have to go inside? Why didn't you just call the fire department?"

I was about to tell Grams that she would've gone in too if she'd seen the fire, only she stands up and says, "And what are we going to do about Daisy? We can't have you *not* go back out, but it's getting so late, and heaven knows when she'll decide to give up for the night."

I look at her kind of doubtful-like. "Do you want me to go over to Marissa's?"

"No, no. That's too far." She thinks for a minute. "How about Dot? Do you think she would mind?"

"She's got a zillion brothers and sisters, and they live in this really skinny house."

"A skinny house?"

"Yeah, and it's—"

Grams closes her eyes and shakes her head. "Never mind about her house. I guess that's out of the question, then?"

"Yeah. Hey, how about Hudson's?"

"Hudson's?"

"Sure! He's got lots of room and a great big couch, and I know he won't mind."

She thinks about this for a minute, then lets out

a big sigh, and off she goes to the kitchen to call. And before you know it, off *I* go to Hudson's with a toothbrush and a change of clothes stuffed in my backpack.

Mrs Graybill's watching all right, but I just pretend I don't know it. I wave bye to Grams and call, "Sorry I forgot my books! See you tomorrow," and head over to Hudson's.

Hudson Graham may be seventy-two, but except for the fact that his hair's all white and his eyebrows need a good raking, it's easy to forget he's that old. He's nowhere near slowing down. As a matter of fact, with Hudson you get the feeling that he's just warming up.

When I got to his house, he was sitting in the dark on the porch, drinking iced tea, thinking. You can always tell when Hudson's thinking because he props his feet up on the railing, crosses them at the ankles, and taps the edges of his boots together like he's listening to music. And since his boots were clicking pretty fast, I knew – he was thinking pretty hard.

He didn't jump up when he saw me coming up the walkway, either. He just reached over to the pitcher, poured me some iced tea, and said, "Hello, Sammy. Have a seat."

What I really wanted to do was take a shower. A

nice long, hot shower. I was tired of being the Marsh Monster, I was sick of the smell of hairspray, and I was cold. But I could tell from the way Hudson's boots were beating each other up that I was going to have to sit there all sticky and green until Hudson had heard the whole story.

I was expecting him to start right in, asking me what I thought I was doing, going into someone else's house and all of that, but instead he says, "So, you've met Chauncy."

That took me by surprise. "How do *you* know him?"

Hudson rocks a bit, then shoos a moth that's fluttering around the brass tip of his boot. "Knew him. Years ago." He nods over at the chair I'm in and says, "He used to sit right there and argue politics with me."

"You're kidding! How'd you meet him?"

Hudson chuckles. "I took an evening course at the college – he was the instructor."

"Chauncy was a *teacher*?"

"That's right. A good one, too. He taught a number of poli. sci. courses there. The kids loved him. He was an eloquent speaker and quite deft at debating – a real champion of liberal causes."

"So what happened?"

Hudson shakes his head. "I don't really know. It

had something to do with the death of his mother. He took care of her until the day she died, and when the will was read, Chauncy wound up with everything."

"Were there other relatives?"

"A brother."

"And the brother didn't get anything?"

"Not one thin dime. Even Chauncy didn't understand it. Apparently Mrs LeBard was annoyed with the brother and didn't care for his wife. Courtney seemed like a fine woman to everyone else, but from what I understand a *saint* wouldn't have been good enough for the mother."

"How come?"

"Who knows? I always figured she had trouble letting go."

We just sit for a minute, and finally I ask, "So where's the brother now?"

"Oh, he still lives in town – off Morrison somewhere. The man's very stubborn. He somehow blames Chauncy for everything – the inheritance, even their mother's death."

"How long ago did Chauncy's mother die?"

Hudson takes a deep breath. "Oh, it's got to be ten years by now. After that, he quit coming over, and pretty soon he started letting the yard go. I used to go over there and offer to help out, but he didn't want it, and after a while he wouldn't even answer the door." Then he says very quietly, "I didn't know about the tracheotomy until tonight."

We both look at the stars for a bit. "Grams says he's dangerous – or unstable, anyway."

Hudson throws his head back and laughs. "Rita told you that?" He takes a deep breath and smooths an eyebrow. "Chauncy is fragile. Brilliant, but fragile. He's an honourable man – he'd go to his grave before he'd hurt another person." He grins at me and says, "I'll have to have a talk with your grandmother about her information sources."

Hudson goes back to staring off into space, and I'm about to ask him if I can *please* take a shower when he says real softly, "How's he doing?"

Well, somehow I don't feel like telling him that this brilliant, honourable friend of his is living like a rat in Vampire Heaven, so I kind of stammer, "Um . . . ah. . ."

Hudson shakes his head. "Rita said he's got no power, no phone. . .? I can't imagine it! That house used to shake with Beethoven and Tchaikovsky. You could smell the coffee brewing from the foyer! How does he make his coffee? Chauncy without coffee . . . can't imagine it! And this time of year . . . he must be freezing."

By now I'm sitting there with my teeth chattering

out of my mouth. Hudson turns to me and says, "You're cold? Say, don't you want to get out of that costume?"

I chatter and laugh and nod all at the same time.

After I take a shower, Hudson brings me some cocoa and shows me to the couch.

When he leaves, I rearrange the cushions, turn off the light, and sit there, snuggled up in a blanket, sipping hot chocolate, and thinking about Chauncy.

But as my eyes get used to the darkness, I start to feel very uncomfortable. See, Hudson's den is really a library. And I'm not talking a set of encyclopedias and a dictionary or two. I'm talking a *library*. He has shelves that go from the floor clear to the ceiling, and whenever I come over with a question that he can't answer, we come to the den and he finds a book that'll tell us.

And I've always liked coming to the den to watch him dig for answers, but sitting there in the dark with books all around me – all of a sudden I feel like I'm spending the night in Vampire Heaven.

It takes me a while to shake off the creeps, and the last thing I remember thinking before falling asleep is, *Why would anyone want to rob a man who seems to have nothing? Nothing but books.*

Hudson didn't wake me up in the morning; his cooking did. I could smell bacon frying and hear eggs popping on the griddle, and let me tell you, that got me out of bed quicker than oatmeal ever has. And it wasn't until I'd eaten three eggs, six pieces of bacon, and a couple of slices of toast that I noticed the clock on the wall.

I jumped up. "Holy smokes! I'm *late*."

Hudson looks over his shoulder at the clock and says, "You've still got twenty minutes."

"Twenty minutes! It takes me almost twenty to *get* to school!" Now part of me's thinking that it's a done deed. I've got detention with Vice Principal Caan for being late, and that's that. But I run into the den anyway, switch into my school clothes, and yank a brush through my hair, because I'm thinking that maybe, just *maybe* I can make it.

And I've got the couch thrown back together and my junk just about stuffed into my backpack when Hudson walks into the room. "I've got your lunch made and Jester's out front warming up. Whenever you're ready."

I stop stuffing. "You're giving me a ride?"

Hudson grins. "You bet."

Jester seems like a brand-new car because it's so shiny it sparkles, but one look at it and you know it's ancient. It's big with pointy tail lights, whitewall tyres, and a mammoth steering wheel. And it's lavender. Hudson insists that it's "sienna rose", but believe me, it's lavender.

It was fun riding to school in Hudson's car. Every time we came to a stoplight people would kind of look, or nudge the person they were with and point, and when we pulled into the school parking lot some kids came up to me and said, "Cool car!"

So the day was off to a pretty good start, when who comes sneaking up behind me? Heather Acosta and a group of her friends. And what does Rude 'n' Red say? She says, "Who was that? Your *dad*?" Then she turns to her friends, and they all laugh like a pack of hyenas.

I felt like telling her to go somewhere deep and toasty, but instead I turn and walk towards homeroom. Heather walks right behind me, though, mimicking the way I'm walking so her friends will keep on laughing.

I try to ignore her, but I'm getting madder and madder and I really want to whip around and push her over. Then she comes up beside me and says,

"Those shoes are just *divine*. Such a luscious green. Oh, do tell! Where did you get them?"

I'm walking faster and faster, thinking *I* know my high-tops look stupid all sprayed green, but they're my only shoes and I didn't have time to wash them so what was I supposed to do? And I'm about to tell her to shut up when all of a sudden her eyes get really big and she starts to giggle. Then she backs off. Just like that.

I look across the patio to see what Heather's giggling about, and what I see is Amber Bellows charging in our direction. And let me tell you, she is *mad*. I move aside because I don't want to get in her way. I mean, I know Amber because she's the head cheerleader and the eighth-grade president, but Amber doesn't know me from the man in the moon, and I figured there was no way she could be mad at *me*.

Boy, did I figure wrong. She comes right up to me with her nostrils flaring, whips that long brown hair out of her way, and says, "You stop bothering him, do you hear me? I've had enough of this! It's not funny, and it's not cute!"

I point to myself and say, "Me? Stop bothering *who*?"

She wobbles her head a little. "Yeah, right. Like you don't know what I'm talking about." Her neck pushes out so she looks like a vulture. "Jared. Remember Jared? The love of your life? The guy you would *die* for? The one who makes your little heart flutter?"

By now the whole school is watching, and I'm feeling really embarrassed. I mean, Jared Salcido is cute, but he's like someone from another planet to me, and he's sure not someone I'd ever thought about long enough to make my heart flutter. On top of that, I've always thought that Amber and Jared were the perfect little preppy couple, so her little tirade had me completely confused.

Finally, I manage to say, "Amber, I think you've got the wrong person."

She laughs and tosses her hair around some more. "You're Sammy Keyes, aren't you?"

I nod real slow.

"So stop calling him! You're making a *fool* of yourself." And she's about to leave but she just can't help herself: William Rose Junior High School's Student of the Week for about six weeks in a row says, "Nice shoes," then laughs and walks away.

The whole time Amber was yelling at me, this big circle of people around us was quiet. Dead quiet. But the minute she leaves they all start talking and whispering and laughing. And I'm standing there feeling like I just fell off a merry-go-round, when

Heather walks by with her friends chanting, "Sammy loves Jared, Sammy loves Jared."

I would've turned around and gone home right then if Marissa and Dot hadn't run up asking, "What *happened*?"

I say, "I don't *know*," then tell them everything that Amber had said.

When I'm done, Marissa shakes her head and whispers, "That is so weird!"

The bell rings and Dot says, "Don't worry about it, Sammy – you'll straighten things out!" She goes to her homeroom, and off we go to ours, and the whole time we're hearing the announcements and getting our books ready for our classes, Heather's passing notes and the other kids are whispering. Whispering and pointing.

Marissa throws me a note that says WHY DIDN'T YOU WASH THEM?

I want to tell her about Mrs Graybill and about sleeping at Hudson's and waking up late, but I can't. All I can do is sit there in a room full of kids who think I have ugly feet and a crush on Jared Salcido while the rest of the school is busy spreading rumours about me. And what they're saying is, "Sammy? You don't know who *Sammy* is? No problem – she's the one in the green shoes!"

So I suffered through homeroom and then walked

my little green feet over to English where Miss Pilson decided to spend the whole class period talking about this big assembly we're supposed to have in the cafeteria next week. Normally Miss Pilson could give two hoots about assemblies. I've seen her sit at the back with the art teacher, Miss Kuzkowski, and talk through entire assemblies.

But Miss Pilson's interested in *this* assembly because it has to do with English. Some professor of hers from college wrote a book about a farmer in the Midwest, and she invited him to speak to the whole school about it. It's been Professor Yates *this* and Professor Yates *that* for weeks, and, really, she acts like she's crazy in love with a guy who made up a story about someone who ploughs fields.

After English I went to maths, and I started to write a note to Marissa because I couldn't concentrate on what Mr Tiller was doing anyway. Trouble is, Mr Tiller noticed.

Normally I can answer any question Mr Tiller might decide to ask me, and normally Mr Tiller doesn't have to worry that I'm writing notes while he's explaining something. So maybe that's why he just stood there for a second watching me, kind of twitching his moustache back and forth while I gave him half a smile and looked guilty.

Everyone likes Mr Tiller. He's young and funny

and smart, and half the girls in school have a crush on him. The only thing *not* to like about him is that he posts notes. He tacks them up on the bulletin board for everyone to see, and leaves them there for *days*.

Mr Tiller didn't post my note. He didn't even take it away from me. He just said, "Sammy, give me the prime factors for three hundred fifty-seven," and held out the chalk.

I looked at him and said, "Can't I do it at my desk?" because I didn't want to stand in front of the class in my stupid green feet. He just held out the chalk and gave me that get-up-here-*now* look.

So up I went, and sure enough the kids snickered. And I'm standing there trying to break down three fifty-seven and getting nowhere when Mr Tiller says softly, "Is it divisible by two?"

I shake my head.

"Three? Do the digits add up to a multiple of three?"

I nod, and that's all I need. I break it down and write 3 x 7 x 17, then hightail it back to my seat.

Bobby Krandall leans over and says, "Nice shoes."

I say, "Yeah. Matches the snot in your nose, Bob," but really I feel like throwing up.

I was hoping we'd have a few minutes at the end of class to talk so I could go sit with Marissa, but

Mr Tiller lectured clear to the bell, and when it rang he gave us our homework. Then he said, "Could I see you for a minute, Samantha?"

So I stayed put while everyone else left. And while Mr Tiller's erasing the board he says, "I know it's none of my business, Samantha, but I heard a rumour before class. . ."

He turns around and looks at me and, really, I just wanted to put my head down and cry. He comes over and says, "Sammy, look. Maybe you should go talk to someone. One of the counsellors? They might be able to help. I hate to see it affect your work."

I stand up and say, "But Mr Tiller, it isn't *true*. I've never spoken to Jared Salcido in my *life*. I don't know why this is happening!"

Mr Tiller looks pretty surprised. "It's not true?"

Kids for the next class are starting to pile in, and I'm not going to stand there and try to convince him. I just say, "No, it's not!" and leave.

All through history I was dying to talk to Marissa, but since Mr Holgartner moved me across the room from her because we always talk during films, I just sat there trying to figure the whole thing out. *Someone* was calling Jared and it sure wasn't me.

And the more I thought about it, the more I kept coming back to Heather. I mean, why did she go bug-eyed when she saw Amber Bellows coming at us? It's like she *knew*. And the more I thought about that, the more convinced I was that *Heather* had been calling Jared and pretending to be me. And she was saying the stupidest, most embarrassing things she could think of.

Once I figured it out, I didn't feel bad any more. I felt mad. Not a wild kind of mad – a quiet, warm kind of mad. And all of a sudden my shoes didn't matter. So they were green. So what?

I didn't even hear the lunch bell ring. I sat right through it, trying to figure out how I was going to get back at Heather for making me the laughing stock of William Rose Junior High.

Finally Marissa comes up and says, "Sammy, c'mon. Let's go."

We head over to the lunch line, but I don't feel like being a guppy in a bowl of barracudas, so I say, "I'll meet you on the patio, OK?"

Marissa says, "Sammy, come with me. I've got to *talk* to you."

I look at her and say, "What's wrong?" and as I'm following her to the lunch line she whispers, "Mikey tattled."

If you knew Mikey, you'd know that this was not big news. Mikey's the most annoying little brother a person could have, and tattling is what Mikey does best. So I snicker and say, "About what *now*?" but I'm thinking, *I've got bigger stuff to worry about than this.*

She looks at me. "About the sweater."

"What sweater?"

"The green sweater. You know ... the Marsh Monster sweater."

I stare at her, thinking that the last time I saw it, it was lying in the middle of a pile of ashes looking pretty charred. "But you said she never wears it!"

Marissa grabs a tray. "She *doesn't*, but now she's saying how much she loves it, and it turns out it's a Louis d'Trent."

"A Louis d'*What*?"

"It doesn't matter. What matters is the stupid thing cost five hundred bucks."

I almost fell over. Really. I mean, here I'd been, cruising around town as the Marsh Monster in a Louis d'Foo-Foo sweater, liking it because it was so *ugly*, and the whole time I was burning up – what? A hundred dollars an hour?

I grab her by the arm. "What did you tell her?"

Marissa whispers, "I told her you still had it and you'd bring it back this weekend."

"You told her *what*? It's ruined, Marissa! I put out a *fire* with it, remember?"

She kind of nods, and as she's paying for her

lunch she says, "I was thinking maybe we could get it cleaned or something. I mean, how bad could it be? It wasn't a very *big* fire. Maybe it's just dirty."

I throw my hands up in the air. "It doesn't take a big fire to burn up a sweater! Besides, he's probably already thrown it away!"

Marissa says, "C'mon, Sammy. At least go back to the Bush House and *try*. It's a five-hundred-dollar sweater! Where are we going to come up with five hundred dollars?"

I thought about this and said, "OK. I'll go. Right after school," and as we're walking out to the patio I say to her, "You're going to come with me, aren't you?"

Even when she's walking, Marissa can kind of do the McKenze dance. And my asking about going to the Bush House was making her dance, all right. I look at her and say, "Forget it, Marissa. It's all right. I'll do it by myself."

She dances a little faster. "I'll go. Really, I'll go. It's just that the place gives me the *creeps*."

I laugh and say, "After the day I've been having, the Bush House is going to seem friendly."

All of a sudden Marissa forgets about the sweater. "That's right! What in the world is going *on*?" She looks at me like she's afraid to tell me something. "It's all anyone wants to talk about."

I see Dot waving her root beer at us from the patio, so I kind of steer Marissa towards her, and as we're sitting down I whisper, "I think I've got it figured out."

Dot grabs my arm. "About Amber and Jared?"

"Yeah, about Amber and Jared." I lean in. "Who do you know that hates me so much she would call Jared Salcido and *pretend* to be me? And who do you know that would give her right earlobe to break the two of them up so that maybe *she* could go out with him?"

Marissa looks at Dot and then back at me. "Heather?"

I smile. "Exactly!"

We're all quiet a minute then Dot says, "She wouldn't. . ."

I laugh. "Oh yes she would!"

Marissa whispers, "What are you going to do?"

I unwrap my sandwich and take a nice big bite. And while I'm chewing, I'm smiling. Dot and Marissa grab me and say, "What? What are you thinking?"

"I'm thinking that a good place to start would be to crash Heather's little Halloween party tonight."

Marissa practically chokes on her hamburger. She looks back and forth over her shoulders. "Crash her party! Are you *crazy*? She'll throw you out the door in a hot second and spend the rest of the night laughing about you! That's *all* you need."

I let her think I've lost my marbles for a second, then I lean forward and whisper, "I'm not planning to go as *me*. I could dress up as something I'd never be – like a ballerina or a bunny or something – and then go as, say, Dot's cousin from out of town."

Of course, I don't have a clue what kind of costume I should wear, or even how to get one – there are no tutus hanging in Grams' closet, if you know what I mean. All I know is that it's a great idea if I can only pull it off. So I'm sitting there, looking back and forth from Marissa to Dot, wracking my brains about what I can be, when all of a sudden Dot jumps off the bench and says, "I know! I know!"

Marissa and I say, "What? What?" and pretty soon our noses are all about five centimetres apart and Dot's whispering, "Last year for Halloween I went as a princess! My mom made me this terrific costume with layers and layers of skirts, and a lavender mask with sequins and stars and stuff all over it. You could put on some lipstick and earrings and curl your hair... Heather would never recognize you!"

Marissa and I look at each other and say, "Perfect!"

The rest of the afternoon I didn't listen much to my teachers or even care that people were still whispering about me. I just sat in class, looking forward, thinking about Heather's party and what I should do once I got in the door.

When school was finally over, Marissa and I headed home together – me walking and Marissa riding her bike as slow as she can. And to tell you the truth, I think Marissa forgot all about going over to the Bush House because when we get to the mall she says, "You want to go to the arcade?"

I just say, "Nah. I've got to go by Bargain Books. I promised Grams I'd check on a book she ordered." And really I do. I promised. Then I ask, "Want to come?" even though I know Bargain Books is about the last place Marissa would want to go. Well, the Heavenly Hotel is about *the* last place, but that's another story.

She says, "I think I'll just go over to the mall. Why don't you come by when you're done?"

I almost said, *Why don't* you *come with me to the*

Bush House when I'm *done?* but instead I say, "I'll probably just see you at Dot's around seven, OK?"

She waves and calls, "If we can pull this off tonight, it's going to go down in history!" Then she goes to play video games and I go up Broadway, past Maynard's Market and the Heavenly Hotel, to Mr Bell's bookstore.

Bargain Books isn't like the bookstores you see in the mall. It's *old*. What gives this away is not the coffee stains on the platform where Mr Bell has his register and computer and stuff, and it's not the creaky steps that go up to the loft – they're covered with brand-new carpet. And it's not the miles and miles of used books, because there are pretty new-looking ones, too. No, what gives away the fact that Bargain Books has been around a long, long time is the smell. It's not a bad smell – kind of like wet wood mixed with dry grass. It's just an old smell.

Anyway, I walk in and give my eyes a minute to adjust because it's always dark inside Bargain Books. Dark and cool. When I can see, I notice Mr Bell with a big box chock-full of books saying to a woman, "Did you have more than this in mind?"

The woman's wearing red high heels and really tight blue jeans, which is bad enough, but on her powdered little nose is perched a pair of big, boxy sunglasses that cover up half her face. *Sunglasses*. In

Bargain Books. She says, "A few more, and that should do it."

Mr Bell pulls a few more books off a shelf and piles them into the box. He rings her up and says to me, "I'm sorry, Sammy. I'll be right back," and then off he goes, squinting at the sunlight, carrying this mountain of books out to the woman's car.

When Mr Bell comes back, he's looking pretty frazzled. Not that he ever looks tidy. He's always got a shirt tail sticking out or a sleeve half rolled up, but I think that it's his hair that makes him look a mess, even when the rest of him is trying to be tidy. It looks like dirty cotton balls glued to the sides of his skull. There's not much left of it, but what there is is really fighting to be noticed. Anyhow, while he's standing there blinking, I say, "Who *was* that? Is she really going to read all of those books?"

Mr Bell laughs, "No, Sammy, she's not going to read them. She's going to decorate with them."

"Decorate with them? What do you mean?"

He steps up to his desk area and takes a gulp of his coffee. "Some people think it's posh to have old books on their bookshelves – they think it gives them an aura of intelligence. To them one old book looks like another. They haven't any idea what's valuable and what's junk; they just want to buy up enough books to give them a facade of sophistication." He takes a bite of a half-eaten English muffin. "The only use I have for people like that is they help keep my electricity flowing." He holds out his paper plate and says, "Muffin?" – as if charcoal peeking up through raspberry jam is my idea of a taste sensation.

I just shake my head and say, "No, thanks. I'm here to pick up a book my grandmother ordered. Has it come in?"

He takes another gulp of coffee. "Oh, I meant to check on why that's taking so long. I expected it days ago. Tell you what I'll do – I'll make a few phone calls and get back to you." He shuffles through some papers and says, "Or you can stop by tomorrow, if you'd like. I'll be here all weekend."

So I say, "Fine," and off I go, back into the sunshine. And, really, I wanted to forget all about Marissa's mom's sweater and the Bush House, but I couldn't. Five hundred dollars is more money than I've ever seen, and the thought that I'd used something that cost so much to put out a fire was making my stomach do the Twist.

So I take a deep breath and head over to Orange Street. As I'm walking I notice that a lot of the houses are for sale or for rent. And I start daydreaming about my mom coming back from trying to make it as a movie star and maybe getting a real job and renting all three of us a house. I mean, do you know how nice it would be to come home to a *house*? No Mrs Graybill, no fire escape . . . maybe even my own room? It'd be great!

And I was so busy daydreaming about my own room and how I'd decorate it that I didn't notice that the sun was disappearing. I was smack-dab in the middle of the bush tunnel before I realized it, and what's funny is I wasn't even spooked. When I turned up the Bush House walkway, all those bushes and thorns and branches didn't seem scary; they were just bushes and thorns and branches. And when I passed the part where the Skeleton Man had almost ploughed us over, well, OK, I did think about him, but only for a second. My heart was still doing a nice steady *thub-dub, thub-dub, thub-dub*.

That is, until I got to the front door. I don't know why the front door got my heart slapping around. It's just a door. Sure it's green and splintery and has a rusty old mail slot, but that's the kind of door you'd expect to see on a house that's smothered in bushes.

But my heart was thumping, and I knew if I stood there much longer my knees would start bumping, so I raised my fist and knocked on the door.

Then I stood there, looking at those splinters,

and waited. And when no one answered, I pounded on the door. Then I pounded some more. And all that pounding seemed to make my heart happy, because I could feel it slow down a little.

Still no one answered. But I couldn't exactly leave – there was a five-hundred-dollar sweater inside. And even though it was probably roasted beyond recognition, I still had to see for myself. Chances were one in a million that it could be repaired, but the chances of my coming up with five hundred bucks to replace it were nil. Zippo. I stood there a minute, thinking, and finally I knocked on the door with one knuckle – three fast knocks, three slow knocks, and three more fast knocks. Then I did it again.

After the third try, I put my ear up to the door, trying to hear if there was any movement inside, wondering if for all the books he had, the Bush Man didn't know a simple SOS when he heard one, when I hear this gurgle-growl right behind me.

I jumped, spun and practically fell down. And there's Chauncy, almost smiling.

I take a deep breath. "You *scared* me!"

He gurgles, "Sorry," then motions for me to follow him. "You're . . . in . . . trouble?"

I follow him around the side of the house, through a maze of bushes to the back. And the whole time I'm getting scratched up, thinking there's no way we can *go* any further, he's ducking in and out of bushes without snapping a twig, moving like a fish through coral.

When we get to the back of the house, he motions to a rusty old folding chair that's half sunk in the dirt. So I sit, and right away I notice that next to me on a rusty wrought-iron end table is a pair of binoculars. Good binoculars. Way better than the ones I borrow from Grams.

Chauncy goes behind a hedge and pulls out another chair that's practically welded shut from rust. He stands there pushing and pulling, and finally the thing creaks open. He puts it on the other side of the table and sits down like he's getting into scalding bathwater, and it hits me: Chauncy LeBard *is* a gentleman – I got the good chair.

I guess it was pretty obvious that I was itching to pick up his binoculars because he rearranges his chair, then gurgles, "Go ahead."

I picked them up, and wow! It was like looking through a microscope. And I'm scanning his yard, going up and down and side to side on the bushes when Chauncy makes a little clicking sound with his mouth, and points. I look where he's pointing, but I don't see anything. Then I try with the binoculars, and there, on the very tip of a branch, is the tiniest bird I've ever seen.

Now I've seen birds before – lots of them – crows and pigeons and the pet shop regulars like parrots and parakeets. But I'd never seen a bird like this. It was almost silver – like a real polished grey. And round, as if it were puffing itself up, only it wasn't. It had a black beak and short little black feet, and it didn't seem to fly very well. And I would've thought it was just a chick, but after I watched it fluttering around the biggest, ugliest bushes on earth I realized that it was going back and forth to a nest.

I lower the binoculars to say something to Chauncy, but he's not there. And as I'm turning around to look for him, he comes walking through the back door, flipping through pages of a book. He points to a picture, then hands me the book and starts looking though the binoculars himself.

Normally a book on birds wouldn't have done much for me, but there was something about this tiny little fuzzy thing twittering around Chauncy's bushes that made me want to read all about it. So while Chauncy's checking out Fuzzball, I read the page he's opened for me in *Rare and Exotic Birds* and find out that I've never seen a bird like this before because there are hardly any left. Fuzzball's almost history.

When I finish reading, I really want to *talk* to Chauncy. You know, ask him a bunch of questions like, *What came first? Fuzzball or the bushes?* and *How come you have a nearly extinct bird fluttering around your yard?* But looking at Chauncy I realize that I'm never going to get half my questions answered.

So I'm just sitting there, watching him watch Fuzzball, when all of a sudden there's a sound like a dozen machine guns ripping through the air. I jump right out of that rusty old seat and yell, "What is *that*?"

Chauncy rolls his eyes and points over the side fence. He writes on his notepad RUSS WALLER/CHAINSAW, then he motions me inside the house. When the door is closed up tight, he gurgles, "Russ . . . doesn't like . . . my . . . sanctuary." Then he says, "You . . . needed . . . help?"

So I tell him about being the Marsh Monster and how the ugliest sweater on earth turned out to be a five-hundred-dollar designer disaster and that I need to at least try to get it cleaned and repaired.

He looks at me and you can tell – he wants to ask me a million questions, but all he says is "Come . . . with . . . me."

He still had the sweater, but it wasn't in the

hallway any more. He'd moved it into Vampire Heaven along with the stack of newspapers, right next to the fireplace. And it didn't take a genius to figure out that if I'd put off coming back to the Bush House a day, Louis d'Foo-Foo would've been a pile of designer ashes.

The sweater was hopeless. There were holes burned clear through, and bald spots all over it. And it smelled. Like burned hair.

Chauncy comes over and inspects it with me. He shakes his head and gurgles, "I'm . . . sorry."

I didn't want him to start thinking he should have to pay for the stupid thing, so I tucked it under my arm and tried to change the subject. "Have the police come up with any suspects?"

He gives me kind of a blank look.

"You know – the Skeleton Man. . .?"

"Oh," he mouths, then shakes his head.

"Did you find anything else missing besides the candlesticks and your wallet? That sack he was carrying sure looked like it had more in it than a couple of candlesticks."

He just shakes his head some more.

"Were they valuable? The candlesticks?"

"Senti . . . mental."

Sometimes I know when to keep my mouth shut, but not very often. "Were they your mother's?"

He cocks his head sideways and squints his eyes a bit. "Yes."

"Have you asked Officer Borsch to question your brother?"

His eyes quit squinting – they pop open and drill into me. "Who . . . told . . . you?"

I shift around a little because he's not looking too friendly, let me tell you. I tuck that half-bald sweater under my other arm and say, "Hudson Graham." Then I shuffle around some more and say, "He says you guys used to be friends. He's worried about you. He didn't know about your operation, and all he could talk about was how this place used to shake with music – Beethoven and Tchaikovsky . . . that's what he said. And he's worried about how you make your coffee with no electricity – he said he can't imagine you without your pot of coffee."

Chauncy looks down at his feet. And while he's busy inspecting the missing polish on his oxfords, I say real quietly, "He also told me you and your brother haven't spoken since your mother died. He says she left everything to you."

Both of us are quiet for a minute, and then he looks up. And I don't know what to do, I don't know what to say, because there I am with the Bush Man, and he has *tears* in his eyes. "I . . . tried . . . to give him . . . half. He . . . wouldn't . . . take it." He sits down in the chair I'd found him in on Halloween. "She . . . did me . . . no favours."

"Does he know about your operation?"

He shakes his head. "Please . . . go."

His eyes close, and I can tell – our conversation is over. So the next thing you know I'm back where I started, staring at ugly splinters, wondering if Chauncy LeBard will ever open his door for me again.

I head back down the walkway and turn into the tunnel, and as I'm giving the Marsh Monster sweater one last hopeless look I hear, "You some relation to that LeBard character?"

I jump, and then I see a man carrying a chainsaw. I take a few steps back. "Ah . . . *no*. No, I'm not."

He tosses that chainsaw into his other hand. "What's that you've got there?"

I tuck the sweater back under my arm and say, "It's just a sweater. Look, I'm late getting home . . . Could I get past?"

He doesn't turn around or back out of the tunnel. He comes *towards* me. So what do I do? Well, I don't know what you would've done, but I turned around and *ran*.

Seven

I got through the bush tunnel all right, and when I'm safely out the other end I look over my shoulder and what do I see? Nothing. Mr Chainsaw's gone. Poof! Disappeared.

I cross the street and head back up past his house. I can't see him, but I sure can *hear* him. He's got that chainsaw revved up so the whole neighbourhood's shaking, and let me tell you, I'm not about to stick around to watch him use it.

I started running home because I knew I was late. I didn't know how late until I got to School Street and heard St Mary's tower start to gong. And for a second I just stood there, counting, not quite believing what I'm hearing. I mean, if I'm not home by four o'clock Grams is worried. But *five* o'clock? How did it get to be five o'clock?

So I started running again – well, as much as you can run with a backpack bouncing around on your kidneys and a two-tonne sweater under your arm. Then I decided that the smart thing to do would be to go to Hudson's and call Grams. So when I got to Cypress I hung a left, and sure enough, there's

Hudson on his porch with his feet propped up, shooing a fly off his boots.

He sees me coming and says, "Sammy! Glad you dropped by." Then he notices the sweater. "What've you got there?"

So I hold it up, and while he's circling it like it's some kind of diseased animal I say, "Want to buy it? It's only five hundred bucks."

He looks at me like I'm crazy, so I tell him about Mikey and Marissa's mom and how I used her Louis d'Foo-Foo sweater to put out the Bush Man's fire.

At first Hudson just keeps circling, looking at me, then at the sweater. Then he busts up. Completely. And after a minute of his laughing and slapping his leg and shaking his head, tears are coming out of his eyes and he has to sit down to catch his breath.

So I sit down next to him and look at him real seriously. "Hudson, what I want to know is if you have five hundred dollars I can borrow. I need to replace this."

His laughing kind of sputters to a stop, and then his chin drops. And I let him sit there like a man with a toothache for a minute, before I say, "I'm *joking*. What I really want to know is if I can use your phone to call Grams. I'm late, and she's probably worried."

He's still in a bit of shock over the sweater, but he says, "Sure," and leads me into the house.

Now I knew that telling Grams I'd been watching rare and exotic birds with Chauncy would not exactly fly as an excuse for being so late, but I figured if I told it fast enough I might be able to get *out* of trouble before I was really in it.

Once again, I figured wrong. She kept interrupting me with so many questions that finally I had to say, "Grams! Just let me tell you what happened, would you?"

When I was all done straightening everything out and I was sure she was done being mad at me, I said, "Grams, I have to ask you a favour."

Silence.

"Grams?"

"What is it?"

"The whole school is going to a Halloween party tonight, and I really want to go."

"You went out last night, Samantha."

"I know, but this is really important. I *have* to go."

She was quiet for a minute. "Why do you *have* to go? Whose party is it?"

Well, what am I supposed to do? Lie? Not to Grams. "Uh . . . Heather's."

For a minute I thought the phone went dead. "Heather *Acosta's*?"

"Um . . . yeah."

"But you *hate* Heather Acosta."

"You're right, I do, which is why I have to go!" So I tell her about the miserable day I had being the girl-in-green-shoes-with-a-crush-on-Jared-Salcido and how I've got to prove that Heather's the one making the phone calls.

"But how is sneaking into Heather's party going to help you prove that she's the one behind the phone calls?"

"I don't know yet, Grams. I just know that I can't sit around while she does this to me!"

I could feel her thinking, and after a long silence she says, "*Promise* me you'll be careful. That Heather has an evil streak."

"I know, Grams. That's why I'm going."

I told her goodbye and was about to hang up when she says, "Samantha? Please be careful. And don't go into any strange houses to put out fires tonight, OK? I worry."

"I know you do, Grams. I love you, too." But as I'm hanging up the phone, I'm thinking – I'll be going into a strange house, all right, only it won't be to put *out* a fire. This time, I'll be starting one.

When I got to Dot's house the porch was still full of jack-o'-lanterns, but they were looking a bit limp –

like they were tired of smiling and having moths buzz in and out of their mouths all night. And when I rang the bell, Dot's dad answered the door and *he* looked kind of limp – like he was tired of smiling and having kids buzz in and out of his house all night.

Dot, though, was full of smiles and didn't seem tired at all. She grabbed my arm. "C'mon! I was just about to go up in the attic."

Dot's attic had exactly what an attic is supposed to have – boxes and boxes of junk. And with five kids in the family, believe me, there were boxes and boxes and *boxes* of junk. And I'm banging my head and bumping my elbows and in general just beating myself up trying to follow Dot through this maze of boxes, but I'm happy. I'm in an attic.

It's easy to get sidetracked when you're looking for something in an attic. You start looking for one thing and pretty soon you're finding all sorts of other neat stuff that can keep you busy for hours. And being in someone else's attic – *every*thing's a sidetrack because you've never seen any of it before.

Anyhow, Dot's way ahead of me, saying, "I know it's here someplace. I remember helping Dad label it. I thought it was back here." Then I come across an open box just crammed full of stuff. And maybe

I should've been polite and just ignored it – I mean, going through someone's attic is kind of like going through their chest of drawers. But there it was, and there *I* was, and I couldn't help it – I started nosing.

One of the first things I found was a strange-looking metal funnel with a handle on it. I held it up and said, "Hey, Dot! What's this?"

She looks up from her rooting around. "A meat grinder." She pushes some hair out of her face and says, "Hey, get over here and help me find the box. I think it says 'Halloween' on it."

So I put it back and make my way over to Dot. We look around for a while, but I sure don't see any box marked HALLOWEEN, so I start opening up unmarked boxes, looking for anything that seems vaguely spooky.

I was finding toys and clothes and dishes and stuff, but there wasn't a bat or a witch in sight. And I was starting to feel like I was looking for snow in the desert when Dot calls out, "Here it is!" and yanks open a big box.

As she's pulling out miles of pink and lavender skirts, something in the box I'd been looking through catches my eye. It's kind of like a walkie-talkie, only I'd never seen a pink and white walkie-talkie before. And the two parts didn't look anything alike. One part looked just like you'd expect a little girl's walkie-talkie to look – only I couldn't see where you would *talk* into it. The other part was about twice as big, and it rested in a base with a plug.

Dot's all excited about finding the princess costume, and she's holding it up saying, "Isn't it terrific? This is going to be great!" but by now I *have* to know what this pink and white contraption is. So I ask, "Dot, what *is* this thing?"

She looks over and says, "Oh, that's just a baby monitor."

I've spent zero time around babies, so I don't know what a baby monitor is. I stare at it, and finally I just come out and ask, "What's it *do*?"

Dot picks up all the parts of the princess costume and says, "My mom used to use it when my sister was napping. You know – she could do the dishes and stuff downstairs while my sister was asleep upstairs, and she could hear when my sister gagged or woke up or something."

I sat there staring at it, thinking, and I could feel my heart speed up a little. "Did she ever take it outside? Like when she was gardening or something?"

Dot looks at me like she can't believe I'm still asking questions about a stupid baby monitor. "Sure. All the time."

"Do you think your mom would mind if I borrowed this?"

She shrugs. "Not a bit."

Then I remembered the Louis d'Foo-Foo disaster sitting in a bag downstairs. "What if something happens to it? Is she going to be upset?"

"Hmm . . . I don't think so. She was saying at dinner the other night how she should really get up here and take all the baby stuff down to the Salvation Army. I'll ask her, but I'm sure it's OK." She looks at me and says, "What do you want it for, anyway? You know someone who's going to have a baby?"

I laugh. "No, but I've got a plan and if it works, I know someone who's gonna have a cow!"

Marissa *had* forgotten about going over to the Bush House. At least she'd forgotten until her mother asked her if she'd brought the Marsh Monster sweater home. And when she joined Dot and me in the Land of Yellow, the first thing she asked was, "Did you get it?"

"Oh, I got it all right." I held it up for her to see.

She practically cried. "What are we going to *do*?"

"I guess we'll have to tell her what happened. *I'll* tell her, if you want."

"She is going to *kill* me!"

We spent the next few minutes trying to figure out some way to save Marissa's life, but finally we decided that there wasn't much we could do about it right then, so we got busy changing for Heather's party.

Dot transformed into the Bee, and Marissa decided that she'd rather wear a gypsy costume of Dot's than wrap up in another mountain of toilet paper, and by the time they were dressed we were already an hour late. And since Dot kept insisting that *she* was the one who should put make-up on my face, I just sat there waiting, trying to decide the best way to sneak the monitor into Heather's party.

When the Bee and the Gypsy were done getting ready, they slapped me in a chair by the mirror and got to work. Now it's not that I think girls who wear make-up are wacko or anything, although girls who wear red or blue eyeshadow have a few marbles on the loose. It's just that I don't *like* it. Mascara makes me feel like I've got bird wings up there flapping around, and lipstick makes me feel like I kissed raspberry syrup. And foundation? You can *have* foundation. It's like smearing peanut butter on your face, and if you think I'm walking around with peanut butter on my face, you can think again. Green paint, yeah. Peanut butter? Forget it.

Anyhow, after about fifteen minutes I've got birds flapping on my eyes and syrup on my lips, my hair's knotted up in some kind of genie-do, and they've snapped a pointy little hat with wispy scarves on to my head. And when they slapped that mask on my face, even I didn't recognize me.

Dot wrestles me into ten layers of skirts and then says, "Put these on" as she hands me a pair of ballet slippers.

I can tell by looking at them that they're not going to fit, but wearing my high-tops would be like carrying a banner saying HERE'S SAMMY! So I push and yank and pull a bunch of faces, and then there they are: cute little pink feet at the bottom of *my* legs.

I take the small part of the monitor and snap it inside my tights, then I let down about half of the skirts and say to Marissa, "Hold this up, would you?" I take the big part of the monitor and press it against my side with the antenna facing down and say to Dot, "Can you wrap the cord around my waist?"

When Dot's all done wrapping, I tie the cord off and straighten out the skirts and we all smile at each other, because, really, you can't even tell it's there.

I turn around a couple of times and try on a new voice – a kind of high, cutesy one. "What do you think my name should be? Tiffany? Wendy? Nikki?"

Both of them shout, "Nikki!"

Then Dot says, "Oh! Oh! You're supposed to be my cousin, right?" and before I can answer, she sits me back down in the chair and pulls out her black eyeliner. And very carefully on the bottom of my cheek she paints a dot. Not too big, not too small – just enough so no one will question that Princess Nikki is Dot's relative.

We all look in the mirror and laugh, and I say, "C'mon! We've got a party to crash!"

Heather was dressed up as a bimbo rock star. That crazy red hair of hers was ratted up on top, and she had on enough leather to cover a couch, including a pair of black boots that went up to her knees. And wrapped around all that leather were so many chains and studs and belts, that she looked like a Dobermann pinscher that got tangled up chasing a cat around a tree.

We weren't stupid enough to all go up to her door at once. Marissa waited down the block a few minutes while Dot and I rang the bell. And when Heather answers the door, Dot says, cool as can be, "Hi, Heather. Great outfit!" Then she nods towards me and says, "This is my cousin, Nikki. I hope you don't mind that I brought her. . .?"

Heather looks me up and down. "No, that's great. Come on in." Then she notices my dot and says through all her rock star make-up, "Does *everybody* in your family have one of those?"

Dot looks at me so I try out my Princess Nikki voice. "Every single one of us – even the cats."

Heather gives me a funny look. "The *cats*?"

I grin. "Yeah, we're raising leopards."

At first she thinks I'm serious, but then she starts laughing, and pretty soon we're all busting up over the lamest joke of the year. And when we're all done laughing I say, "Cool earrings," because she's got on the *ugliest* earrings I've ever seen. They look like someone cut a circle out of an inner tube and glued on red marbles.

Heather smiles real big. "Thanks!" She looks at me a little closer and says, "Your name's Nikki? You're all right."

Just then the doorbell rings and, sure enough, it's Marissa. Heather says, "Well, well, Marissa. I didn't think you'd show up without that loser friend of yours. What's she doing tonight? Painting her shoes?"

Marissa does a bit of the McKenze dance and looks around. "Wow, this is some party!"

And it was. There were people everywhere. Heather's house is kind of spread out and has lots of wood panelling and scrap metal sculptures hanging on the walls – copper windmills and birds and stuff like that. And the further into the house we wandered, the more rooms there seemed to be, and every single one of them was packed with kids from school. I'm not talking just seventh graders. There were eighth graders, too. *Lots* of them.

And part of me's feeling kind of bad. Here are all

these people, having a good time, *liking* Heather Acosta, and I'm the one person in the entire school that Heather hates. It doesn't matter to them *why* she hates me; all they know is that Heather hates this girl named Sammy, and anyone who could give such a terrific party must be right. Not that it makes any sense; it's just the way that kids who don't think about things think.

So I'm wandering around with Dot, looking at everyone eating Halloween cookies, feeling like a cat in a dog kennel, when all of a sudden Heather comes up behind me and says, "Hey, did you get some punch?"

I hate to admit it, but I didn't see her coming. And hearing Heather's voice right there in my ear made me jump. On top of that, it was weird having Heather be *nice* to me, so after I get done jumping I kind of stand there batting my wings through the holes in my mask. "What?"

She laughs. "C'mon. There's punch and cookies and stuff in the kitchen. Want some?"

I say, "Sure," and then Princess Nikki kicks back into gear. "I'm starved!"

Dot and Heather and I are all heading towards the kitchen, and I can tell from the way Heather's looking at me that she's ready to start asking me questions. So I say, "This is an awesome party,

Heather. I can't believe how many people are here. You must be really popular!"

That makes her smile real big. And she's about to say something like, *No joke!* when this lady comes out of the kitchen calling, "Heather! Heather, bring me some towels, would you? The punch spilled."

At first I thought this woman was something out of a weird sixties movie. She had hair the colour of a new penny, and it swooped right over her left eyebrow, clear around her head, and into a monster beehive.

And that was just her *head.* On her body she was wearing a hot pink scoop-neck blouse with sleeves that looked like little pink petticoats. And green spandex pants. I'm talking *lime* green. And on her feet were gold high heels with big fake jewels going across the tops.

Then I noticed the dainty sapphire necklace that she was wearing, and it slowly dawned on me that this was not a woman in costume. This was Heather's mom.

So I'm standing there taking all this in, when Heather says, "C'mon."

I make myself quit staring at her mother and follow her down the hallway. And when Heather sees that Dot is coming with us she says, "Why don't you go talk to Marissa, Dotty? She looks lonely."

I turn towards Dot and roll my eyes, but before

you know it I'm going down the back hallway alone with the Dobermann.

Heather gets some towels from a closet near the end of the hall, and then opens the door to a room nearby. She says, "Give me just a sec," then goes over to a full-length mirror and plays with her hair and rearranges her chains a bit while I stand in the doorway watching.

It doesn't take me long to figure out that this is Heather's bedroom. There are posters all over the walls – mostly of pop stars and movie stars. Her bed's not very big, but it looks big because it's got a king-size black-and-white fuzzy cowhide bedspread hanging clear down to the floor. An end table by the bed is covered with the same material, and sitting on it is a music box and a thirty-centimetre-tall plastic cow. And I'm wondering what the deal is with *cows* when I realize that the one on her end table isn't just a knick-knack – it's a phone.

I guess Heather saw me staring at all her cow stuff because she says, "I used to think it was cool, but now I'm sick of it. I'm trying to talk my mom into letting me redo my room, but she's being her usual tight self."

"Your mom seems pretty cool to me. . ."

Heather snickers. "My mom's a joke. She's forty

years old, and I swear she thinks she can still pick up twenty-year-olds." She blows some air out the side of her mouth. "She's probably out there right now, flirting with an *eighth* grader." Then she laughs and says, "With my luck she's trying to pick up Jared."

I can't resist. "Jared? Is that your boyfriend?"

That makes her little chains jingle. "Don't I *wish*. No, but he's the cutest guy at school, and knowing my mom, she's probably out there asking him to dance."

I didn't think I could ever laugh at anything Heather Acosta said, but the thought of Heather's mom with her tornado top and spandex bottom dancing with Mr Cool was enough to make *anyone* laugh, even me.

And when I started laughing, so did Heather. So there we are, the worst enemies in school, cracking up together. When we wind down I ask, "So why don't *you* go ask him to dance?"

She crosses her eyes. "Because *Amber's* here."

"Amber?"

"His girlfriend. She is such a witch. No one can even *talk* to Jared without her grabbing his arm and trying to get him alone. I wish I could – " A smile spreads across her face. "C'mon." Then she does something that makes every hair on my body shoot straight out. She links up with me. She's got the towels in one arm, and she links her other arm through mine and yanks me along. And I'm stammering, "What...? Wait..." but the next thing you know she's delivered the towels to her mother and we're in the den, standing in front of Jared and Amber.

Jared's dressed up like a baseball player, and he's slouched on the couch looking pretty bored. Amber's perched on the armrest, with the tail of her cat costume and one arm wrapped over his shoulders.

Heather says over the music, "Hi, guys! Are you having a good time?"

They nod, but you can tell – they're not.

"This is my friend Nikki."

They barely look at me. "Hi."

So we stand there, looking around, and Heather says, "So why aren't you dancing?"

Jared shrugs. Amber twitches her tail.

"You're not letting this Sammy thing get to you, are you?"

Jared snickers. "*I'm* not."

Amber hits him with her tail.

I pipe up with, "What Sammy thing?"

Heather laughs. "Sammy..." She looks at Jared. "What can you say about Sammy?"

Jared just laughs through his nose and shrugs, but Amber puffs out like a cat ready to fight. "Well, I can tell you this – she's strange."

Jared grins. "But she's got good taste."

Amber whacks him with her tail again.

"How's she strange?" I ask. Like I really want to know.

Amber rolls her eyes. "She wears green shoes, for one thing."

"And she's got the hots for Jared, for another." Heather winks at Jared and says, "Not that *that's* so strange. She just won't leave him alone."

Jared smiles back at her, and Amber's so back-combed about *me* that she doesn't even notice what's going on right beneath her whiskers.

I ask, "Seriously?"

"Seriously. She's been making harassing phone calls, and from what I understand, they're pretty embarrassing!"

Amber shakes her head. "Where does she get the *nerve*?"

"That's Sammy for you."

My stomach's churning like a cement truck. It feels sick and heavy, like it's going to slosh over any minute. And as Heather sets me up, bit by bit, I know that what I've got to do is get *away* from her so I can get to work on my plan, but I can't just leave. I've got to stand there and smile while this ball of cement sets up in my stomach.

I say, "Sounds like you don't like her very much, either."

Heather laughs and says, "What's there to like? She's nosy and sneaky, and she thinks she's *so* smart." She grins at Amber. "But at least she's not horning in on *my* boyfriend."

Amber stands up. "Can we talk about something else?" She holds out a paw to Jared and says, "I'm ready to dance now."

Jared takes her hand but gives Heather a sly little wink as he walks away.

That about sends Heather into orbit. She grabs me by the arm and shakes me. "Did you see that? Did you see the look he gave me?" She keeps on shaking. "It's working! It's working!"

Well, I knew darn well what was working, but I probably would've asked her anyway just to see if she'd tell me or not, only I couldn't. I was afraid to move, let alone breathe. See, with all that shaking Heather was doing, the cord of the monitor had slipped loose and I could feel it, slithering like a snake down my body.

I grab my side and say, "Uh, I really need to use the bathroom. Can you tell me where it is?"

She's got her eye on Jared. "Oh, sure. It's down that

hall where the towels were. First door on the left."

I smile and say, "Thanks," and then hobble my way over to the bathroom as fast as I can.

The minute I'm inside I lock the bathroom door and let go of the cord, and – *thunk!* – the big part of the baby monitor falls to the floor. I tuck the thing under my arm, then I check the hallway, and sneak my way down to Heather's room.

The light was on, so I clicked it off and peeked out her window to see which way the bedroom faced. I was relieved to see streetlights – at least I wouldn't have to go snooping in her backyard later.

I turned the light on again and started searching for a place to plug in the monitor. I decided the only place that would work was under the bed. Trouble is, I couldn't reach the outlet without crawling under the bed. So there I am, with fifteen princess skirts tangling me up and the scarves from my pointy little hat falling in my face, trying to reach the outlet, when all of a sudden I hear the door open.

I scrunch the rest of the way under the bed and hold my breath. Then I hear Heather say, "Come on!"

I can't see who she's talking to because I'm surrounded by polyester cowhide, but when I hear this fake baby-girl voice say, "Does she ever come in without knocking?" I know she's with Monet Jarlsberg.

Monet sounds like a Barbie doll with a mosquito stuck up her nose. And the fact that she's Heather's little pipeline to the cool crowd makes her annoying *and* sneaky. Really, considering how many people Monet's stabbed in the back, I'm surprised she's lived as long as she has.

Anyway, I hear their footsteps getting closer and closer to the bed, and all of a sudden Heather is groping around *under* the bed, saying, "Nah. Anyway, she's too busy mixing up more punch."

Now my heart's having a banging good time with my chest, and I'm doing my best to inch away from Heather's hand when I notice a pack of cigarettes peeking out from under the corner of her bedspread.

Her hand's hopping around like a frog on a griddle and she's saying, "They were right here!" and I know if I don't do something quick, she's going to *look* for them, and then Princess Nikki will be busted. So I scoot the pack of cigarettes a few centimetres closer to her, and when her hand hops on to them, *whoosh!* they disappear.

I let out a big sigh, but the next thing you know

Heather and Monet are flopping on to Heather's bed. And they don't just sit there. They *bounce*. And every time they do, the box spring crushes my shoulder, and no matter how I try to move, here comes the bed, smashing me like a giant princess tenderizer.

When they settle down, I hear Heather say, "Here. I don't get my allowance till next Friday, so I'll give you the rest then."

"That's what you said *last* time, and you never did."

By now I've pulled the corner of the bedspread aside so I can hear better, and I can smell cigarettes burning away up there. Heather blows out smoke. "Oh, c'mon, Monet. You didn't have anything *good* last time. If you've got something good, I'll get you the rest on Friday."

Monet starts to argue, but then she sputters and spits and starts hacking away like she's going to die. And there goes the bed again, bouncing up and down, turning me into a princess patty.

Heather laughs. "I thought you said you did this all the time!"

"I do!" Monet tries another puff, but pretty soon she's hacking again.

Heather says, "Just tell me what you heard, would you?"

Monet says through her coughing, "What do you want first – Jared and Amber, or Sammy?"

And then I remembered – Monet had been sitting one table over at lunch when we'd been talking about crashing Heather's party.

So now I'm pulverized *and* worried. Real worried. What if Monet knew I was planning to crash the party? I didn't think we'd been loud enough for anyone to hear, but we were excited and maybe someone *had* heard. Especially if that someone had been paid to listen.

So there I am, suffocating under polyester cowhide, dying to know if I should leave Heather's party through a window or not, when Heather says, "Jared and Amber."

Monet giggles. "Amber is *mad*."

"At Sammy?"

"A little at Sammy, but more at Jared."

"Why? He can't help it that that loser Sammy's all gooey over him."

Monet squeaks, "'Cause he's eating it up! I heard Amber tell Jill that all he does is talk about his 'animal magnetism' and how he's powerless to stop her. She told Jill that it's turning him into an egomaniac. Can you believe it? Like his ego could've got any bigger."

Heather doesn't say anything for a minute. Then she asks, "You think she's going to break up with him?"

"Oh, who knows? You saw her out there in your living room – she's like glued to him. Gag me." Then she laughs. "Maybe if *Sammy* was here. . ."

Heather snickers and says, "So tell me about Sammy."

There goes my heart again, *ka-boom, ka-boom, ka-boom*. Monet says, "She's *real* upset about everyone teasing her about Jared. What an idiot! Did she think it wouldn't get around?" She coughs a couple of times and says, "She's gotta be kinda weird. I mean, who would paint their shoes *green*?"

Heather snickers some more. Now normally I'd want to pop out from under the bed and tell Monet to shoot bug spray up her nose, but for some reason it's easy just to lie there with a box spring in my face, listening. And the more I listen, the more I understand that breaking up Amber and Jared and framing *me* for it is so important to Heather that she hasn't told anyone about it. No one knows what Heather's up to.

No one but me.

And no one is going to be able to get me out of the mess I'm in.

No one but me.

Nine

I was so relieved that Monet hadn't overheard anything about my plan to crash the party, that when Heather stuffed the cigarette pack back under her bed it didn't even faze me. And after they got done hosing the room down with air freshener and marched out the door, there I was, under Heather Acosta's bed, all alone.

I didn't waste any time. I popped the monitor's plug into the outlet and clicked on the switch. Then I pulled myself out from under that polyester cow, straightened out my costume, turned the key of Heather's music box a few times, and sneaked back to the bathroom.

Once I'd locked myself in the bathroom, I took out the other half of the monitor and turned it on. And when I heard music coming through that pink and white receiver, I did a little princess victory dance.

When the music started slowing down, I turned the monitor off, stuffed it into my tights, straightened myself out, and headed back to the party.

I hadn't been in the living room more than thirty

seconds when Dot comes buzzing over and whispers, "Where have you *been*?"

Marissa comes up behind me. "Did you do it?"

I smile and nod. "It's a done deed."

Anyone looking at us would've known we were up to something because Marissa's and Dot's eyes are bugged way out, and we're huddled up like football players. So I take a step back and try to act like I'm talking about homework. "You know Monet Jarlsberg? Guess who's been *paying* her to spy on people?"

They look at each other and then back at me. "Heather?"

I nod, and Dot says, "She's been *paying* her?"

"That's right, and guess who she was spying on today at lunch?"

Dot fades into an albino bee. "Does she *know*?"

"No, but I'm ready to get out of here. How about you?"

So we're about to head for the door when Marissa whispers, "Your dot's running."

It takes me a second to realize what she's talking about. I blot my cheek with the back of my hand and, sure enough, there's eyeliner smeared on it. I say, "Is that better?"

"No, it's worse!"

Dot's busy trying to fix it when all of a sudden

Marissa takes off. And as I'm wondering where she's going, my ears hear something that my brain's not quite receiving. It's kind of like when Grams is waking me up to go to school: "Samantha . . . Samantha . . . say, Samantha, it's time to get up. . ." But it's not Grams' voice I'm hearing, and it's not "Samantha" that's drifting into my brain. It's "Nikki . . . Nikki . . . hey, Nikki! What's going on?"

When I finally figure out that it's Heather talking to me, I slap a hand over my cheek like I'm busy thinking and squeak, "Um . . . well, actually, we've got to get going. But it sure was a great party!"

"Already?"

"Yeah, sorry. I had the best time, though." I giggle and tilt my head and let the scarf on my pointy hat drape in front of my face a bit. Then, because it seems like she's going to ask me something else, I say, "And those are still the coolest earrings I've ever seen. Where'd you get 'em?"

Heather prances around in her leather and chains. "At the mall." Then she whispers, "They were only two bucks."

"No way!"

And you're not going to believe this, but she pulls them off her earlobes, *snap, snap*, and hands them to me.

I keep my cheek covered up while I say, "No,

really, I can't." But before you know it I'm standing there holding the ugliest earrings on earth, saying, "Heather, you're something else."

My feet had absolutely no problem finding their way to the door or down the street. And by the time Dot and I got to the end of the block I was so relieved to be *out* of there that I just stood on the kerb for a minute, looking at the moon, wondering how long it would take for Heather to figure out who Princess Nikki really was.

By the time we had all met back at Dot's and got out of our costumes, it was pretty late. And when Dot's dad found out that Marissa and I were planning to walk home, he insisted on driving us instead. I had him drop me off at a house two blocks from the Senior Highrise, and then ran the rest of the way home.

When I walked through the door Grams was half-asleep on the couch, but she didn't stay that way for long. She made me tell her all about the party, and even though she kept one hand in front of her mouth, underneath it I could see a smile. And when I was all done, she couldn't help it any more. She busted up.

When she's all done laughing, she puts her arm around me and says very seriously, "Samantha, I know that growing up isn't easy. Even for kids like Heather, who make it *look* easy – it's just not. And it's too bad that people like Heather have to make it rough on people like you, but I want you to know I'm proud of you for not taking her shenanigans lying down." She looks at my feet and says, "I've also been thinking that there are a few things I could do to make life a little easier on you. I think it's high time we went out for a decent pair of shoes."

I nod and say, "I do want another pair of shoes, Grams, but if I get another pair now, Heather's going to know that she got to me. I don't *want* green shoes, but if I get another pair now, she'll think *she's* the reason."

Grams frowns. "Are you sure?"

"I'm sure."

I must have been really tired because I don't really remember getting ready for bed. I do sort of remember Grams easing off my shoes and tucking me in, but the next thing I know I'm waking up to sunshine and the jingling of keys.

I look up, and there's Grams, coming through the door with a basket full of folded laundry, and perched on top of it are my green shoes. "Sorry for waking you, dear."

"Where are you going with those?"

"Where I've *been* is to the basement. And I've

spent the last hour and a half in the laundry room trying to get these things to come clean. I prewashed them – I bleached them. It's hopeless, Samantha. I know you're attached to them, but look here – they're practically worn through on the bottom." She puts down the laundry basket with a thud. "Heather or no Heather, it's time I took you to the mall for a pair of real shoes."

"Grams, no! Not the mall!"

"Why not the mall? They have perfectly good shoes at the mall."

Grams may act like she accepts my high-tops, but not-so-deep-down inside she hates them. Green or not. If she had her way, my poor little toes would be covered in buckles and bows. And buckles and bows or not, I *hate* new shoes. They pinch your toes and bite your heels and rub you raw until they're finally broken in, and then they're not *new* any more. Why pay all this money for new shoes and have your feet feel like they've been gnawed on by a grizzly bear, when there are shoes out there that have already gnawed up somebody *else's* feet and are ready to start being nice?

So I jump up and say, "But they're expensive! Why don't I just take the SMAT bus over to the Thrift Store and look for a pair there."

"Another pair of . . . *those*?"

"Grams, high-tops are the best. They're comfortable, they last a long time, and they're only a few bucks over at the Thrift Store."

She's sighs. "Well, they're practical, I suppose. They're just not very ladylike."

So we sit down to a hearty breakfast of oatmeal and grapefruit, and after we've cleaned up, Grams digs through her purse and hands me a ten, a five and five ones. "Is this going to be enough for bus fare and shoes?"

"It's plenty, Grams. Thanks." So off I go, over to the mall to catch the SMAT bus.

Santa Martina doesn't have big city buses. We've got little ones, like shuttle buses. They look like dog carriers for people, if you ask me, but they're actually pretty nice inside. Sometimes there's a bum or two kind of passed out in the back, but usually I sit up close to the driver.

I was the only one waiting at the bus stop when it showed up, and since there were only a couple of other people on board, I got to sit right behind the driver.

So, we're roaring around town, having a good time stopping at bus stops and pumping diesel exhaust into the air, when I see a sign for Morrison Street. And we're about two blocks past Morrison when I remember that Hudson had said Chauncy's

106

brother lived somewhere near Morrison Street. So I'm turning around, trying to see something that's already long gone, when the bus driver comes squeaking up to a red light and says in the mirror, "Something wrong?"

I know it's not a bus stop, but the bus is stopped, so I jump up and say, "I've got to get off here."

He pushes his hat back and scratches what's left of his hair. "I can't do that."

"But I . . . I . . . I'm. . ." I open my eyes wide and hold my stomach. "I'm gonna barf!"

He slams that door open, and I'm off faster than a bull at a rodeo. After he zooms away, I cross over to a gas station and dig through the phone book at the payphone. There was only one LeBard listed, so I figured that LEBARD, D.W., 123 ELM CT. must be Chauncy's brother.

I didn't know where Elm Court was so I went up and asked the gas station attendant. He points back down Broadway with his squeegee and says, "Take a right on Morrison. You'll run right into it."

So off I go down Broadway, and when I hit Morrison I take a right and, sure enough, there's Elm Court.

Elm goes way around in a circle. It's like the world's biggest cul-de-sac with an island of houses in the middle. Some of the houses have peaky-pointy roofs and look like little doll's houses from Denmark, and some of the houses have flat roofs and look like little adobe forts, but all of them are really tidy and have perfect little yards.

Number 123 was one of the doll's houses. And it was different from the other doll's houses not because of the yard – it was perfect just like the rest of them – but because the yard had grass and nothing else. No trees, no flowers, no vines. No bushes.

I didn't really know what I was doing there. Part of me wanted to go up and ask Chauncy's brother a bunch of questions, and part of me thought it was the stupidest idea I'd had in a *long* time and just wanted to head out to the Thrift Store. Before you know it, though, I'm on the porch, pushing the doorbell.

Nobody answers. And I'm turning around to leave when a man and a woman decked out in white cotton and carrying tennis rackets come walking towards the house.

They stare at me and I stare at them, and the man says, "May I help you?"

There's no doubt about it – this is Chauncy's brother. He's a bit taller and healthier-looking than Chauncy, but his *eyes* are what give it away. They're a clear brown, like toffee-coloured marbles. And sharp, like he knows what you're thinking before you've even had a chance to finish thinking it.

"Mr LeBard?"

He looks straight at me. "Yes, and you are. . .?"

I stick out my hand. "Samantha Keyes."

While he's shaking my hand, he never takes his eyes off me. I try to keep looking straight at him, too, but it's hard – like looking at the sun.

"Chauncy was robbed the other night. I thought you might want to know."

He looks at me like he doesn't quite believe what he's hearing. He leans his head forward a little, then squints and says, "He sent you here, didn't he? Well, you just tell him I'm not interested in this ploy of his. If I've told him once, I've told him a hundred times – I'm through with him. I want nothing to do with him!"

I squint right back at him. "He did *not* send me. I just thought you might want to know."

"Well, I don't!"

"Wait a minute, would you? Hudson says you guys used to be really close and—"

"I do *not* want to hear any more of this. You tell that busybody Hudson Graham to mind his own business!"

Up until now Mrs LeBard has just been standing

there, watching and listening, but when her husband starts getting all worked up she holds him by the arm and says softly, "Douglas, give the girl a chance to talk. It's been almost ten years. Life doesn't go on for ever, you know."

While he's busy thinking about telling her to stay out of it, I say, "He didn't want the inheritance, you know. He said that your mother did him no favours."

Ol' Douglas turns on me. "I'm sure charming Chauncy has told you a lot of things. He may think he can talk his way out of any situation, but this is one time his vocabulary isn't going to do him any good. I'm not listening!"

That's when I realize – he doesn't know. "You're wrong, Mr LeBard. Chauncy hasn't talked to me very much at all. He can't. He's had a tracheotomy."

That stops him cold. His wife says to me, "When, dear? When did this happen?"

I shrug and say, "It must have been quite a while ago, but I don't really know. All I know is he's living without heat or electricity or a phone or anything, and he can't talk."

The Mr and the Mrs are looking at each other, just kind of letting this sink in, and finally the Mrs says, "Without heat or electricity? What about the inheritance? He can't possibly have used it all up! Why, the appraiser said that—"

Douglas cuts her off, saying, "Never mind about that! If he's spent it all, he deserves to suffer, and if he didn't learn his lesson from what happened to Mother, it's his own doing."

I look at Mrs LeBard and ask, "What happened to their mother?"

She says softly, "She died of lung cancer, dear. Douglas tried for years to get them both to quit but—"

"Courtney, that's enough! It's none of her business, and the whole matter is no longer any of our concern. If he's been sick, I can't help that. If he's spent the inheritance, then so be it."

"Excuse me, but it doesn't look like he's spent money on much of anything. Maybe if you went over there and talked to him—"

That does it. Douglas says, "Don't tell me what to do, and don't stand there expecting me to justify the situation to you!" He pushes past me, "Out of the way, out of the way!"

Mrs LeBard follows him and looks over at me from the porch, but it's pretty obvious from the way the door slams shut that she won't be inviting me in for butter cookies.

I just stand there on their walkway like a statue,

thinking. And pretty soon my brain's whirring around inside my skull so fast that I can't stand there any more; I've got to get moving.

So I head out to Broadway, hang a left, and start walking to the Thrift Store. And while I'm walking, my brain's busy chasing something that keeps slipping away. It feels like I'm trying to snag a fish out of the water – every time I grab for it I miss, because it's not really where it seems to be at all.

I have to wait for the light on Stowell Road, so I close my eyes and try to imagine the scene on Halloween night. I pretend that I'm Chauncy, with my hands and feet tied and a big rubber mask over my face. Pretty soon my heart's speeding up and I'm feeling claustrophobic and I can't *breathe*. And that's when it hits me: maybe whoever robbed Chauncy LeBard didn't know he'd had his operation. Maybe the Frankenstein mask was more than just a blindfold. Maybe the Skeleton Man didn't know that it *wouldn't* stop him from breathing. Maybe, just maybe, whoever robbed Chauncy LeBard wanted something so badly that he was willing to kill for it.

Either that, or maybe he just plain wanted Chauncy dead.

I don't know why, but the thought that the Skeleton Man might have been trying to kill Chauncy kind of stunned me. I mean, the way I'd been looking at it was that he was after some*thing*, not some*one*. And I was so dazed that I didn't even notice that the light had turned green until it was switching back to red.

When the stoplight turned green again, I started running. Past gas stations and shops and about a mile of strip malls, and when I came huffing and puffing up to the Thrift Store, I felt a lot better. Like I'd outrun the Skeleton Man – at least for the moment.

The Thrift Store doesn't usually have much in it that I like. It has lots of clothes that are OK, I guess. They don't have tags that try to bite you, and at least they're not going to shrink. I mean, if it's at the Thrift Store, there's nothing you can do with a washing machine that's going to make it any smaller.

The trouble with Thrift Store clothes is they're a little strange. They have pinks next to oranges, if you know what I mean. And flowers. Lots of flowers. And if you *do* find something that has OK colours and no flowers, it's probably made of polyester or plastic. Either that or it has zippers and buttons where zippers and buttons don't belong.

So I went straight past all the racks of clothes to the back of the store where the shoes are. Most of the shoes are worse than the clothes. They've got pilgrim shoes and platform shoes and shoes that look like they've been worn by a duck, but in between all these ugly shoes they've also got high-tops. Really great high-tops. And I noticed a terrific pair of black and white ones right away.

Trouble is, they were about an inch too big. I tried them on anyway, thinking that maybe I could wear two pairs of socks until I grew into them, but one lap around the shoe rack told me it'd be like wearing flippers.

I flopped around in the black-and-whites looking for another pair, but all I could find that might've fitted me was a pair of plaid ones – red and pink plaid.

So I took another lap around the rack, thinking that maybe I could get used to the flippers, but finally I just sat down and switched back into my green ones.

I headed for the door, zipping right past lamps

and books and toasters and mixers, but then I noticed something. I wasn't being real observant or anything, I was thinking about *shoes*, you know? I just noticed them because there they were, all alone, decorating the middle of a black Formica table.

They weren't silver, and they weren't stainless steel or aluminum. They were just a dull grey, and kind of rough. But the longer I looked at them, the more sure I became – these were Chauncy's candlesticks.

I didn't touch them for a long time. I just moved around the table telling myself, *Nah! It can't be. . .* Then I got the idea to trace around the base of the candlesticks. I knew the lady at the register wasn't going to offer me a Magic Marker to scribble up her table, so I used the next best thing – spit. I got my finger good and wet and went around the base of a candlestick, making a nice shiny outline on that old black table. And when I picked up the candlestick and looked at my little spit tracing, well, I couldn't say for *sure*, but the design in the dust at Chauncy's house and the spit spot seemed to be about the same size and shape.

I flipped the candlestick over, and there was the price – $10.75 for the pair. Which was about $10.75 more than I wanted to pay for a pair of candlesticks that might never have seen the inside of the Bush House.

So I marched them right up to the cash register. Right up to CeCe.

Most people think CeCe's a little strange, but I happen to know she's sharp like paper. She looks like a bag lady, and I've heard people say she used to *be* a bag lady, only she was so good at collecting stuff that she had to open a store just to have somewhere to put it all.

Bag lady or not, she's like a walking commercial for her store. She wears hats and scarves and lots of orange and pink polyester with jewellery dangling everywhere. And every time I've gone into the Thrift Store she's been friendly to me – like she remembers me even though I only go there a few times a year.

She looks at me over the top of her glasses. "Didn't have your size?"

At first I didn't know what she was talking about – I was thinking about the candlesticks. Then I realize she must have been watching me do laps in her shoe department. "No." I look down at my Marsh Monster shoes. "And if I don't find a pair soon, my grams is going to force me to go to the *mall*."

CeCe wrinkles her nose in sympathy and then

looks over the counter at my feet. "Too bad they're worn out. That's a beaut of a colour."

I look at her and start to laugh, but then I can tell she's serious so I switch the subject. "How long have you had these candlesticks?"

She looks at them through the bottom part of her glasses, and her eyebrows disappear under her fringe. "They're new. Why do you want to know?"

I'm trying to come up with something that isn't a complete lie, when CeCe looks at me straight through the middle of her glasses and says, "Ah-ah. Out with it."

I take a deep breath and say, "It's important. They might've belonged to a friend of mine."

She chews on this a minute. "Wouldn't know about that. They were a donation. Got dropped off in the box outside."

Hearing that gets my heart thumping around a bit. "Was there anything else with them?"

She squints at me, then nods towards the appliance table. "They were in a sack with a toaster. Sucker had a loose wire's all. Fixed it up and buffed it out. It's good as new."

Now my brain's whirring and clacking, thinking *Rats!* because if she hadn't cleaned it up maybe there'd be fingerprints. "Which toaster was it?"

She walks over to the table and picks one up. "You act like a cop, you know that?"

I look it over and see an $8.50 sticker on the side. "Can I borrow this and the candlesticks for a day?"

She tosses her head back and laughs. "Oh, that's a good one. I suppose next you're going to tell me they're stolen property. I've heard that one before." She goes back to the register and settles on to her stool. "And no, I won't come off the price any."

So I stand around trying to figure out some way around paying for stuff I don't even want, when she taps the ALL SALES FINAL sign behind her. "Don't be gettin' any bright ideas, girl."

I sigh and say, "Look, I've only got about nineteen, and with tax—"

She perks right up. "Cash? Forget the tax. I'll refigure. We'll call it an even nineteen, if that's all you've got."

She tucks the money away in one of her polyester pockets, puts the candlesticks and the toaster in a paper sack, and says, "Come back any time!"

It didn't take me long to figure out that I'd been an idiot for giving CeCe all the money I had. Now I couldn't ride the bus. Instead I had to trudge along

Broadway with my green shoes and nineteen-dollar sack of junk.

The whole time I'm walking, I'm thinking. And what I'm thinking is, before I go home or even over to Hudson's, I've *got* to go to Chauncy's and see if this is his stuff. So when I get over to Stowell Road, I hang a right and keep on walking until I get to Miller Street. Then I walk and walk and walk some more until finally there's Orange Street.

And I walked down Orange Street like I didn't have a care in the world. I picked up a stick and ran it across Chauncy's neighbour's picket fence, slapped the FOR SALE sign with it, and then poked my way through the bush tunnel and right up to Chauncy's door like I'd done it a hundred times before. My heart wasn't thumping, my knees weren't bumping; I just pounded on the door and hollered, "Chauncy! Open up! Hey, Chauncy, it's Sammy! Open up!"

But he didn't open up. And pretty soon I'm tired of banging my fist on his splinters, and I'm thinking that maybe he can't hear me because he's out back watching Fuzzball.

So around back I go, ducking branches and thorns like I own the place, and, sure enough, there's Chauncy, up to his forehead in binoculars. And since the rusty old chair he'd used the last time I visited was still out, I just sat down and waited.

And waited and waited. And when he finally takes the binoculars down and looks at me, he says, "You're ... per ... sistent" – the way most people would say, *You stink*.

I just smile at him and pop a candlestick on his rusty little table. "This yours?"

At first he stares at it, then he stares at me. Then he picks it up like it's made of crystal instead of tin, and he nods as he turns it over and over.

I tug the other one out of the sack. "Are you *sure* they're yours?"

He holds them both and nods a bit faster.

So I pull out the toaster and say, "How about this?"

Well a toaster was about the last thing Chauncy expected me to pull out of my little bag of tricks. He scratches his head. "Where ... have ... you ... *been*?"

So I told him everything. Including how it had cost me nearly twenty bucks to get his stuff out of CeCe's store.

The minute he hears about the money, what's he do? He reaches into his back pocket and pulls out his wallet. And while he's piecing together twenty bucks, my eyes kind of bug out and I say, "When'd you get your wallet back?"

He hands me the money, then flips his wallet closed. "Police. Found . . . near . . . mall."

I think about this a minute. "Was anything missing from it?"

Chauncy shakes his head no.

"Was Officer Borsch the one who brought it back?"

He nods.

"Did he have anything else to say – like who their suspects are?"

"No."

I kind of mumble, "Figures," and for a split second I thought I saw a little twinkle in Chauncy's eye, but it was gone before it was really there.

We sit a minute, and then I ask, "Have you found anything else missing? *Any*thing?"

There goes his head again, shaking back and forth.

"Well have you *looked*?"

He gives me half a shrug and looks the other way.

Now with all this shaking and shrugging he's doing, I'm getting pretty frustrated. So I take the toaster and stuff it back into the sack and say, "OK, you tell me – why would someone come into your house and steal some stuff he didn't want?"

He looks down at his feet and shrugs.

I say real quietly, "The Skeleton Man was trying to kill you, wasn't he?"

For a long time he just sits there, but finally he shrugs.

"You think it was your brother, don't you?"

He jumps to his feet and starts pacing back and forth, shaking his head. "Why . . . now? Why . . . the . . . disguise?" He sits back down, motions to the candlesticks, and says, "Thank . . . you," then puts his head in his hands.

I can tell that he wants to be left alone, so I pick up the sack and go out the way I came. And I'm about halfway home when I decide that home is not where I should be going.

The police station is.

Eleven

I didn't *want* another conversation with Officer Borsch, but I didn't know what else to do. The toaster had to be connected to the Skeleton Man somehow, but *I* sure didn't know how.

And I'm walking along, thinking about killers and toasters and how Chauncy would probably rather die than tell the police that he thinks his brother tried to do him in, when I notice these two men arguing on the other side of the street.

I know it's none of my business what these two guys are pointing and yelling about, but I slow way down anyway, and pretty soon I'm practically stopped, listening to them. They're both about the same age, but one of them looks like he changes oil for a living, and the other – well, I'd bet what's left of my high-tops that he has a closet full of ties and a cell phone in his car.

Mr Cell Phone's yelling, "Look, park them in your garage, park them in your driveway, put them down the street somewhere, but don't put them in front of my house! You're breaking an ordinance and you know it. This is not commercial property. If you want to run a used car lot, rent yourself a spot across town!"

I look around and, sure enough, there are about ten old beat-up cars right around the Oil Man's house. He wipes his hands on a rag. "I ain't breaking any ordinance. You've had the cops down here so many times you ought to know that by now."

"That's because you move them right before they get here!" Cell Phone rubs his forehead and says, "Look. *Please*. I'm trying to sell this house, and it just won't move with your cars parked out front."

Oil Man sneers and says, "Sorry, buddy. That's your problem, not mine," then walks away.

You can tell from the way Cell Phone's hands are turning into fists that he'd like to *make* it his problem, but he just marches back up to his own house and slams the door.

I start walking again, and I'm about a block from the police station when something starts rattling around in my brain. At first it's kind of quiet – just a little rumble. But before you know it, it's like a gorilla up there, shaking a cage. And when the cage busts open, I quit walking to the police station and cut over to the mall to find a phone booth.

I flip through the estate agents section of the yellow pages, trying to remember the name on the sign. I know it's Sunrise or Sunshine ...

Sun-*something*, so I keep on looking until I find it: Sunset Realty.

When a woman answers the phone, I pinch my nose and say, "There's a house on Orange Street? Six twenty-nine East Orange? Can you tell me a little about it?"

I listen to her it's-a-darling-three-bedroom-starter-home-with-the-feel-of-real-country-living spiel, and when she comes up for air I ask, "Has it been on the market long?"

What does she say? Nothing. Absolutely nothing. I slap the phone and say, "Hello? Are you still there?"

"Um, yes. I'm sorry. What was that?"

"Has it been on the market long?"

"A little while, yes, but the price I quoted you is ten thousand *under* the fair market price. The seller is definitely motivated. Would you like to arrange a walk-through?"

The last thing I want is a tour of Mr Chainsaw's house, so I pinch my nose again and say, "Let me discuss this with my husband first." Then while she's trying to get my name and number I say, "Would you mind telling me something about the neighbour first?"

"The neighbour?"

"You know – the one with the bushes?"

She just sighs. "I don't know what the situation is

125

over there. Look. It's a darling house. I'm sure you'd fall in love with it if you'd just take a walk-through. I could meet you over there in half an hour if you'd like. . ."

I tell her I'll have to get back to her, and hang up the phone. Then I head back across the street to the police station. And as I'm crossing over the police station driveway, a squad car comes bouncing up and practically runs me down.

I'm about to say, "Hey! Watch it!" when I realize that it's Officer Borsch behind the wheel – acting like he doesn't see me.

I wave my arm back and forth, but he's still looking right through me. Finally he starts to manoeuvre the car around me, but I move over a few steps and block his way again.

Muscles is sitting next to him, and he motions me to move aside. I hold up the paper sack and call, "I've got something to show you!"

Officer Borsch whips off his sunglasses, throws them on the dash, and hollers, "I told you to stay out of it!" because he knows I'm not there to show him my groceries.

"But I've got some evidence!"

Officer Borsch tries to rub away a headache while Muscles squeezes himself out of the passenger seat and says, "Let's talk inside the station."

Muscles escorts me in, and when Officer Borsch joins us a minute later, he takes me straight down the hall and practically throws me into an interrogation room. And while he's hiking up his pants and straightening out his gun belt he says, "Sit down," like he's spitting tobacco.

I sit all right, but I roll my eyes at Muscles and whisper, "That breath needs *Lysol*."

Muscles tries to keep a straight face, but you can tell – he's thought the same thing himself. More than once. And in the split second he gives me a smile, Officer Borsch is all over him. "What was that?"

Muscles says, "Nothing, sir. She just ... she just..." and you can tell from the way his jaw muscles are popping around that he's about to shoot himself in the foot.

I jump in. "Look, I walked here from clear across town. All I want's a drink of water. What's the big deal?"

Officer Borsch stares at his partner with those squinty little eyes of his. Then he throws his head a fraction of a centimetre to one side and Muscles runs off to get me some water.

At first Officer Borsch walks back and forth like a caged lion. Then he leans against the table on his fingertips and says, "Do you know what I've been through because of you? Do you have any *idea*?"

I look down, because the last time I got tangled up in one of Officer Borsch's cases, he got into some pretty serious trouble. "I'm just trying to help."

"I've been on the force twenty-six years. Twenty-six years! And after that business over at the Heavenly Hotel, Jacobson tried to force me into an early retirement. When I refused, he stuck me in this lousy rotation with that ... that. . ." and he's dying to say *moron*, but he just can't do it. If there's one person Officer Borsch hates more than his new partner, it's me.

I was starting to get a little nervous. Being in a room with Officer Borsch sizzling and spraying at you is like being in a microwave with a sausage – it's just a matter of time before things get real messy. So I was relieved when Muscles came back carrying cups of water. He had three of them: one in each hand and one in his mouth. He hands one to Officer Borsch and says, "So, where are we?"

Officer Borsch looks up at this fluorescent light that's flickering away, takes a deep breath, and says, "What *evidence* do you have for us?"

So I take the toaster out of the sack and put it on

the table. And the minute I did, I knew I should've told him the whole story first and then brought out the toaster, because right away Officer Borsch wags his head and says, "Well, looky here. She's found us the smokin' toaster!"

Now I felt like packing up my appliance and going home, but I didn't. I closed my eyes, took a deep breath, and said, "If you'd please just *listen*. . ."

Muscles says, "Go on, Sammy. Tell us your story."

So I told them about going to the Thrift Store and how I'd noticed the candlesticks and found out from CeCe that they'd been left with the toaster in the donation box.

Muscles is looking pretty interested, but all Officer Borsch says is, "So where are the candlesticks?"

I told him about going over to Chauncy's and how he was so happy to get them back.

"And the toaster?"

"It's not his."

Officer Borsch says, "So his wallet's been recovered, and he's got his candlesticks back. I guess all his property has been recovered" – like, *OK, case closed.*

I say kind of quietly, "This toaster is connected somehow to the Skeleton Man. I don't know how, but since this is starting to look like more than just a robbery, somebody should look into it."

Muscles says, "What do you mean, more than a robbery?"

"I think that maybe the Skeleton Man was trying to kill Chauncy."

Officer Borsch rolls his eyes, throws his hands up in the air, and mutters, "Why me?"

I almost left. But Muscles put a hand up and said, "It's been a long day, Sammy. Tell us why you think this, but try to stick to the point, OK?"

So I tell them about my suffocation theory and about Chauncy's brother and the inheritance and how Douglas didn't know his brother had had a tracheotomy. And the whole time I'm talking I'm thinking that when Chauncy finds out what I've done, he's going to want to kill *me*.

When I'm finished, I look over at Muscles and he's busy pushing back his cuticles, nodding away like *Wow, this is making a lot of sense.*

So I say, "There's someone else you might want to investigate."

Muscles says, "And who is that?"

"Chauncy's neighbour. Did you know he has his house up for sale?"

Officer Borsch snickers, "Can't blame him for *that*. But what's that got to do with anything?"

So I tell them about Mr Chainsaw and how

130

Chauncy had said he wasn't too fond of his "sanctuary". Then I tell them about my call to Sunset Realty and how I was sure that the house had been for sale for a long, long time.

They both just stand there for a minute, then Muscles says, "Does his neighbour know about the operation?"

"I don't know."

Officer Borsch says, "So we've got a brother stiffed out of an inheritance and a neighbour who can't sell a house. Is that it?"

I shrug. "It's a place to start."

He shifts around a bit and says, "We'll look into it."

Right.

But there's not much else I can do. So I hand the toaster to Muscles and whisper, "Don't let him throw it away."

When I got back to the Senior Highrise, I went up the back way, as usual, and I peeked down the hall for Mrs Graybill, as usual. But for once her apartment door was closed.

So I hurried down the hall, and I would've just popped right into Grams' apartment, only as I'm putting the key in the lock I hear something I can't believe. I tiptoe over to Mrs Graybill's door and put my ear against it. And there it is: music.

I stand there listening to the sound of violins

and cellos floating out of Mrs Graybill's apartment and I wonder, What is going on? I mean, hearing music through Daisy Graybill's door is like watching your cat eat broccoli – it's just not something you expect to happen.

I wanted to knock on the door, just to see if it was really Mrs Graybill inside, but instead I turned around and went into my own apartment. I closed the door tight and called, "Grams! I'm home!"

Grams calls back from the kitchen, "In here!" and when I round the corner she holds up a finger and says into the phone, "OK, then. I'll see you tonight. Bye-bye."

When she hangs up I say, "Wow, Grams, got a hot date?"

That makes her blush. "Watch your tongue, young lady." She adjusts her glasses and looks at me like she's checking the ingredients of a box of cereal. "Mr Graham has invited us both over for dinner, so don't you get any strange ideas."

Well, it *did* seem a little strange to me, but to tell you the truth I didn't spend much time thinking about it. I had other things on my mind. Like the Borsch-man and the Bush Man.

And exactly what I should stuff into my backpack, so that after dinner I could get to work nailing Heather Acosta with her own lie.

Twelve

You'd think that with the monitor under her bed and all, it would have been easy to catch Heather in the Lie, but it wasn't. First of all I had to get a tape recorder. Grams didn't have one, and I didn't really want to borrow Marissa's. It's about the size of an ice chest and has detachable speakers – not exactly made for covert operations.

Besides, Marissa couldn't even go. Her mom was making her and Mikey go out to the Landmark for dinner so she could show off to some new clients how her kids knew which one of the fourteen forks to use when. I can see taking Marissa, but Mikey? He'll be shooting peas across the room and tripping the guy with the dessert tray before anyone's salted their filet mignon.

Dot couldn't go, either, so I didn't even bother to ask her about a tape recorder. I asked Hudson.

The trouble with asking Hudson was that I had to do it in front of Grams. And even though she understood about Heather, I really didn't think Grams would let me do what I was planning to do.

Sure enough, she asked, "What do you need with a tape recorder?"

I kind of smiled at her and said, "It's for a research project, Grams." It sounded good to me.

She didn't buy it. "Research? For what?"

"For school, Grams. I need it for school."

I could tell the next question was going to be, *For what* class? but Hudson came to my rescue. "You bet I have one. What kind do you need?"

"It doesn't really matter. Anything that works."

He takes me into his study and starts pulling recorders out of a drawer. "I've got micro, standard, reel-to-reel. . ." – and before you know it, his desk is covered with tape recorders and cords and little microphones. He stops and looks at me. "You, ah, probably don't want to be encumbered by a power cord, am I right?"

My mouth gives me away with a little smile.

"Perhaps size is an issue?"

"It can't be *too* big."

He nods like he knows exactly what I'm going to be doing with his tape recorder, and as I watch him I get the feeling that Hudson has all these recording devices not so he can listen to music or seminars, but because he's spent a lot of time *spying* on people.

And I'm about to ask him if that *is* why he has so many recorders, but a little corner of my brain is telling me that if I ask him, he'll turn right around and ask *me*. So, when he hands me a tape recorder that's not much bigger than a bar of soap and says, "This one should do the trick," I take it and say, "It's perfect!"

He digs through another drawer until he finds a tape, then says, "You'll be needing some fresh batteries, too. Let me see what I've got." He disappears and comes back a minute later with two AA cells and then assembles the recorder for me. He hands it over with a twinkle in his eye. "The perfect research implement. And now, how about a piece of pecan pie?"

I ate my pie in two seconds flat. And while Grams and Hudson are chatting and nibbling on theirs, I'm playing with the recorder, getting used to pushing the right buttons without looking. The last thing I want is to be in the dark pushing the *wrong* buttons when Heather's in the middle of pretending to be me.

After dessert Hudson says, "You know, it's a beautiful night out. Why don't we all go for a walk?"

I say, "I can't. I've got to get going on my research, but you go ahead."

Grams gives me a worried look. "But—"

I say, "Don't worry, Grams. I'll be fine. I'll just see you back at home later, OK?"

"You still haven't told me what this research is for, Samantha."

"For school, Grams!"

Hudson interrupts Grams before her next question even starts. "Sammy seems like a very responsible young lady to me. I think we should let her do her research, and I think you should join me in an evening constitutional. It always does me good, and I'd sure enjoy the company."

Grams studies us for a second, then nods and says, "Well, at least you're doing homework. I was beginning to wonder if they weren't assigning any, or if you just weren't doing it."

It was true. I hadn't spent any time doing homework in days. But I couldn't exactly go home and crack the books now. I had real work to do! So I just said, "See you soon," gave her a quick kiss on the cheek, and hurried out the door.

It *was* a nice night out. It was clear, and the moon was like a little white saucer up there, trying to scoop up stars. I kept looking up at it as I walked, and it almost felt like I had company on my way to Heather's house.

The minute I got to the row of oleander bushes by Heather's fence, I took a quick look around, then dived right in.

If Grams had seen me do this, she would've had

a fit. Not just because I was hiding in someone else's bushes, but because the bushes I was hiding in were poisonous. Not poisonous like poison oak or something; poisonous like wild mushrooms, where if you *eat* them, you'll be more than sorry.

I wasn't planning to snack on oleander, though, so it didn't bother me a bit. I just looked around for signs of anyone else nearby, and when I was sure I was alone, I scooted along the fence until I was behind a bush near Heather's window.

I pulled the monitor out of the backpack and turned it on. I played with the volume a bit, then took out the tape recorder and tested it a couple of times just to make sure it was working right. Then I huddled up and waited.

And waited and waited and waited. And let me tell you, in no time I'm *cold*. And after about an hour I'm shivering, my teeth are chattering, and inside my green shoes my toes are turning blue. And I'm starting to think that maybe the monitor isn't working right or that maybe I'm out of range, because all I can hear is some soft static.

Then the phone rings. And I mean *rings*. I jump and bang my head on a branch, and as fast as I can I turn the monitor way down. After about the seventh ring, the light comes on in Heather's room and I hear her say, "Hello...? Hello?" but I guess whoever called got tired of waiting because Heather slams down the phone, and then her room goes dark again.

I should've gone home right then, but I didn't. I sat there, getting colder and colder until I couldn't stand it any more. When I finally decided to give up, I strapped on my backpack and started running. I ran all the way home, and by the time I was letting myself into the apartment, I was *almost* warm.

I was expecting to get scolded for being late, but when I checked Grams' room she wasn't even home yet. I brushed my teeth and shook the leaves out of my hair, and just as I was snuggling up on the couch, Grams comes in the door.

I mumble "hi" like I've been asleep for hours.

She whispers, "Go back to sleep, dear. I'll talk to you in the morning." Then she disappears into her room.

The next day, all I could think about was stupid Heather Acosta and how if I didn't catch her making a phone call I'd be the poor-little-girl-with-the-crush-on-Jared-Salcido until I died. And I guess I wasn't looking too happy, because around lunchtime Grams says, "You look bored to tears, Samantha. Don't you have a paper to write for school or something?"

"A paper?"

"You said you were doing research. . .?"

"Oh, that. Yeah. Um, it's kind of a big project. I'm going to try to get together with Marissa and Dot tonight to finish it up."

I could tell Grams was going to ask me some more questions about my research paper, so I jumped up and said, "Hey, I told Mr Bell that I'd check back about your book. I think I'll go see if it's in."

She mutters to herself a minute, then waves a hand. "Go."

And I was already out the door and halfway down the hall when I realized there was something kind of strange about Mrs Graybill's door. I mean, it was closed all the way, which was strange enough, but sticking out from under her door was the corner of a yellow envelope.

I probably should've just kept on walking, but I didn't. I went clear back to Mrs Graybill's door, and before you know it I'm sneaking that envelope out from underneath it. It looked like some kind of greeting card, and written across the envelope in handwriting like a ghost's was *Miss Daisy*.

I hadn't looked at the envelope for more than two seconds when Miss Daisy opens her door. She stands there with her hands on her hips, looking like the Mrs Graybill I'm used to; she's all bundled up in her dirty pink bathrobe with her hair sticking straight up in back, looking very cranky.

Well, I blushed. Completely. I mean, the reason I think Mrs Graybill is such a pain in the neck is because she's always sticking her nose into my business, and here I am, fishing mail out from under *her* door. And all of a sudden I can see myself in fifty years, looking out my window with binoculars, or peeking out my front door at people going by.

And that's when I get this *awful* revelation: Daisy Graybill hasn't always been a crabby old lady in a dirty pink bathrobe with hair sticking up in back. When she was young she might have been a lot like *me*.

A thought like that can send shivers shooting all through you. And a thought like that can leave you with not much to say. I just stood there with my cheeks on fire and held the envelope out to her. "Here. I'm sorry."

I was expecting her to fly into a rampage about how I have no business being in the apartment building and how she's going to have the manager arrest me, but she just snatched the card and slammed the door.

I stared at her apartment number trying to shake off the picture of me in Mrs Graybill's house slippers, but after a minute I turned around and headed for Bargain Books.

When I walked in, the first thing I heard was Mr Bell cussing. He sees me and says, "Oh, Sammy, I'm sorry. I didn't know you were there."

"Is something wrong?"

He pushes up a sleeve that falls right back down. "Oh, it's nothing." Then he looks at me with a sigh and says, "It's just this bank statement. I'm trying to get my finances in order so I can sell this place but –" He slaps around on his desk some. "I can't even find a pen!"

I stand there a minute wondering if he's serious or not. I mean, Mr Bell is one of those people that's always been around, so you expect him to keep right on being around. It'd be like Father Mayhew saying he was quitting the Church after thirty years at St Mary's.

"*Sell* the place? Are you serious?"

"Yes, I am." He lets out a sigh and says, "How am I supposed to compete with the mall stores? The majority of people that come in here are ne'er-do-wells and bums. Respectable folks wind up going to the mall. I've put my whole life into this place, and what have I got? Negatives in my account." He puts both hands on his desk and leans forward a bit. "I want to sell it, all right. The only trouble is finding a buyer." He lets out a laugh that doesn't sound at all funny. "You know anybody who might be interested in investing in a very used bookstore?"

I study him, wondering if he's serious or just having a very bad day. Then I say, "If you really want to sell it, Hudson Graham might be interested. He loves books. Him or Chauncy LeBard."

All of a sudden Mr Bell gets real quiet. He squints at me. "So you know Hudson Graham."

"Sure. He's got more books than anyone I know – except Chauncy, that is. Do you know Chauncy LeBard?"

Mr Bell shakes his head. "Don't let that Hudson fool you."

"What do you mean?"

He frowns. "Just watch your back."

Before I can ask him what he means, he opens the door and rushes me out. "I'm going to call it a day," he says, and then bolts the door from the inside, leaving me to watch his CLOSED sign swing back and forth.

I stand there feeling pretty strange, and all I can think about is Hudson and what in the world he did to make Mr Bell think he was a backstabber. And since it was obvious Mr Bell didn't want to talk about it, I figured I'd go ask the only other person who would know.

Thirteen

Hudson thought it was funny. "He's still sore about that?" He kicked his feet up on the porch railing. "I guess Tommy's never going to forgive me for that one."

It seemed kind of strange, hearing Mr Bell called Tommy. I'd never thought of him having a first name other than Mister. "Forgive you for *what*?"

Hudson smiles and looks way out over the rooftops across the street. "Do you know what a first edition is?"

"A first-edition what?"

"Well, in this case, book. It's the first run a publisher makes on a book. Sometimes it's a real small run; the publisher decides to print up only a small number of books and see how it does. If the run sells out, they print up more. Sometimes a book that the publisher doesn't expect to do very well becomes popular, and in those cases the first-edition copies can become pretty valuable – and the more rare they are, the more valuable they become." He looks over at me. "Got it?"

"Got it."

He goes back to looking over rooftops. "If you

143

happen to find a valuable first-edition book that's also been autographed by the author, well, that makes it worth more. In some cases, a *lot* more.

"Now it just so happens that I was at Tommy's store once when this fellow came in with a couple of boxes of books. That kind of thing happens all the time at Tommy's. Someone'll clean out his attic and haul all his old books over there, and Tommy'll go through them and say yea or nay to buying them. Sometimes he'll just buy the whole lot for twenty bucks or something.

"Anyhow, I used to stop in quite a lot – have coffee and English muffins and just shoot the breeze – and one day this fellow comes in with a box of books. You could tell from looking at it that it was just filled with trashy old paperbacks. And since Tommy was in kind of a foul mood anyway, he just snorts, 'No thanks,' and goes back to rearranging shelves. So the guy turns to me and says, 'I hauled these things all the way down here – I sure don't want to haul them back. Do *you* want them? You can just *have* them.' So I say, 'Sure,' thinking that I'll do the guy a favour and dump them in the trash out back.

"He leaves, and I start going through the books, and what do I find? A first-edition Heinlein, and it's autographed. Now when Tommy discovers what I've got, he insists that the book is *his* and – well, to make a long story short, he threw me out of his store and I've been banned from coming back ever since."

"How much is the book worth?"

"Oh, to the right buyer a few hundred bucks, but in a few years it may be worth several thousand – who knows? I've got a number of first editions, but that one's my favourite." He shoos a fly off his boot. "So how'd the investigation go last night?" He grins at me and says, "Oh, I'm sorry – *research*."

I scowl and say, "Crummy. I sat out in the freezing cold all night for nothing."

His eyebrows pop up a little. "You're not giving up, are you?"

I sit up in my chair. "No way!" Then I say, "As a matter of fact, can I use your phone?" and before you know it I've talked to Marissa and Dot and they've both promised to come freeze in Heather's bushes with me that night.

When I get off the phone, Hudson comes into the room and says, "Do you think your grandmother would like to go to see a movie tonight?"

I say, "I think you might be able to talk her into that," which is true – Grams never gets to go to the movies. And I'm hoping that he can, because if he takes Grams to the movies, it will be that much easier for me to snoop at Heather's. I've got plenty to worry about without having to worry about Grams worrying about *me*.

So he calls her up and twists her arm, and I race home to get ready for another big night in Heather's bushes.

That night I wore a sweatshirt *and* a jacket, and I only had to wait about ten minutes before Marissa and Dot showed up. We went crashing through oleander until we were real close to Heather's bedroom window, and then we tried to get comfortable.

Now, Marissa's not big on bugs. And since bushes and bugs usually go together, I was kind of surprised when she said she'd go. And she did squirm around a bit, but after a while she calmed down, and the three of us just sat there, whispering and waiting.

And waiting and waiting some more. Finally Dot says, "Maybe we should ring the doorbell or something. You know – stir things up?"

Marissa says, "Yeah. What if she's not even home?"

That got me thinking. I mean, I was pretty sure she was home, but I didn't want to wait all night for her to quit watching TV or reading *Earring*

146

Magazine or whatever Heather Acosta does when she's sitting around at home. Then I got an idea. I groped around in my pockets for some change and said, "Stay right here. I'll be back in about five minutes. If you hear anything happen, start the recorder!"

I ran down the street and locked myself in the payphone booth. Then I pawed though the A's in the phone book, and when I got to Acosta, well, big surprise – Heather's got her own private listing.

I pop the coins into the phone and when Heather picks up and says, "Hello?" my heart's hopping around in places it does not belong.

"Hi, Egg Breath, this is Sammy."

"*What*?"

"You heard me, it's Sammy. I found out you were dogging me pretty good at your little Halloween party the other night, but I've got news for you. People are sick to death of you, your rusty hair and your rotten-egg breath. I wish you could take a whiff of it yourself 'cause you'd probably keel over and die. So do the world a favour and keep your polluted mouth shut. You hear me, Egg Breath?"

Before she has a chance to hang up on me, I slam down the phone. Then I race back to the oleander bushes and, sure enough, the red light's on and the tape is rolling.

Marissa whispers in my ear, "She's in there ranting and raving about rotten eggs!"

Just then I hear Heather's voice come over the monitor. "Who does that stupid Sammy Keyes think she is? Telling me I've got egg breath. . . She thinks she's got news for me, *ha!* I've got news for *her.* Nobody calls Heather Acosta names and gets away with it – *nobody.*" For a second all you can hear is a bunch of drawers slamming and her muttering, and she says, "I guess I'll just have to give Amber a little reason to beat her up *for* me."

I look at Dot and Marissa and pump my fist. "*Yes!*"

We're all so excited that it's really hard not to make any noise, but when we hear her say, "Jared?" we get quiet all right. We don't even *breathe.*

And I can just see her, sitting on the edge of her cow bed, pinching her nose, pretending to be me, not sounding a *thing* like me. And thinking that Jared Salcido could fall for Heather's stupid trick – well, let's just say that a donkey's got parts that are smarter than him.

"Hi, Jared," she says. "This is Sammy. Don't tell Amber I called, OK? I just had to. I love you so much. Will you *please* just give me a chance? Amber doesn't appreciate you like I would. . ."

Jared must've said something really stupid, because Heather laughs real loud and says, "What is she, your mother?" Then after a second she says, "Well, OK. I have to go anyway. I gotta go paint my shoes. Bye!" and hangs up. Then she lets out a real ugly laugh and says, "Sammy Keyes, that'll teach you to call *me* Egg Breath!"

Now we couldn't just pack up and *leave*. We had to play back the recording a couple of times and then make plans for exposing Heather at school the next day.

When we had it all ironed out, we sneaked back out to the sidewalk and slapped hands one last time. And as I'm heading home, a giant giggle comes out of me because for once, I can't *wait* for school.

Don't get me wrong. I didn't get there early. I slid into homeroom right when the bell rang, and the whole time we were listening to the announcements and saluting the flag and getting our books ready for our morning classes I tried my best not to look at Heather. But after Mrs Ambler finishes talking to us and taking roll, Heather leans over and hisses, "You got a lot of nerve calling my house and insulting me. I know you're just sore because you missed the party of the century."

I couldn't help it – I cracked up. I tried to stop, but I just couldn't.

She says, "What are you laughing at?"

I giggled and said, "I heard your *mom* was the entertainment. She was hitting on eighth graders or something?"

"*What?* Who told you that?" She puffs up like she's going to punch my lights out, but the truth is, she doesn't know how. Heather's the sneak-up-from-behind-and-stick-you-in-the-butt-with-a-pin kind of fighter, if you know what I mean. So all Heather can think to do is pull my hair. And it hurts, all right, but I still can't stop laughing.

So she's yanking me out of my desk by my hair and I'm cracking up, and the rest of homeroom's staring at us wondering what in the world is going on. Mrs Ambler hollers, "Ladies, ladies! What are you *doing?*"

I wipe away a tear and try to straighten out. "Nothing, ma'am."

"Nothing?"

"All I did was ask her what she had for breakfast."

The minute I say that, there's a big snicker from across the room, and I know it's Marissa. But I don't look over there like Mrs Ambler does. I just keep right on looking straight at her with a nice little smile on my face.

"And *why* did you want to know what she had for breakfast?"

I shrug. "Her breath smells like eggs, that's all."

Heather cries, "*What?*"

I look at her and say, "Well it *does*, Heather."

Mrs Ambler says, "Samantha!" but just then the bell rings so she shakes her head and lets us all stampede out the door.

I might as well not even have *been* in school for all the attention I paid in my classes. I did listen for a minute in English when Miss Pilson gave us instructions about going to the assembly for her college professor during the last hour of the day, but I have no idea what else she said. All I could think about was Hudson's tape recorder in my pocket, and what was on the tape inside it.

In maths, though, I forced myself to pay attention. Mr Tiller was mad at me because I told him I couldn't find my homework, and the whole time he called out the answers he kept one eye on me. And after every problem he'd work out on the board he'd ask, "Questions?" and look straight at *me*.

And you better believe I paid attention because he'd say, "Jesse, what should I do next?" or "Frances, what's the product of these numbers?" And every time he asked someone to help him work out a problem, he'd start off by looking at *me*. So on the last problem, when he finally does ask me a question, I tell him how to do the whole thing. He finishes writing on the board and says, "See what you can do when you put your mind to it?"

I thought I was off the hook, but when the bell rings and everyone else charges out of class, Mr Tiller calls out, "Samantha! Up here a moment, please."

So up I go.

He takes a deep breath, and when he gets done blowing it out he says, "You didn't even *do* your homework, did you?"

I just shake my head. "No, sir."

He inhales again and then sits down on the edge of his desk with a sigh. "Sammy, I see your grade slipping. I don't like it. You have serious potential, and I want to see you live up to it." He scratches the side of his head and says, "I think maybe it's time I called a parent conference."

"No! Mr Tiller – really. I'm sorry I didn't do my homework. I *promise* you it won't happen again. It's just that . . . well, there's been a lot going on." I look up at him and say, "After today everything's going to start being normal again. Really."

152

He eyes me. "What's so special about today?"

There goes my stupid mouth again, smiling away. I kind of back away from him. "I can't tell you right now, but you'll see." Then I run out the door and call over my shoulder, "I'll have my homework in tomorrow – promise!"

As I'm turning the corner I can see him kind of shaking his head, and you can tell he's thinking, *Teenagers*.

But what *I'm* thinking is that if Marissa, Dot and I can pull off what we have planned for the assembly, Mr Tiller might still have a few questions he wants to ask me – but he'll have a whole lot more for Heather Acosta.

Fourteen

Mr Tiller was at the assembly, and so were the rest of the teachers – guarding the doors, making sure all us kids sat where we were supposed to sit and didn't pop our gum or talk too loud.

Miss Pilson was up front by the podium, fluttering around, gushing over Professor Yates, and when she turned the microphone on and said, "Everyone find a seat now and settle down. Come on, now, settle down!" well, we all kept right on talking about how Professor Yates looked more like a professional yodeller than a writer. He was wearing a waistcoat *and* a sweater, and hiking boots with red laces. On top of that, he was carrying this thing that looked like a walking stick. He belonged in the Alps somewhere, not in a junior high cafeteria.

So we're all busy giggling, calling him Yates the Yodeller, when Miss Pilson taps the microphone and says, "That's quite enough. We need to begin, so, please, can we have it quiet?"

A lot of us did shut up, but it was still pretty noisy until Professor Yates flipped his walking stick upside down in front of the microphone.

All of a sudden the cafeteria's full of the sound of

rain. Really. Rain. And pretty soon no one's saying a word. And when the rain stops, Professor Yates says into the microphone, "Good afternoon, boys and girls. My name's Dr Martin Yates, and this is a rain stick. It's made from a cactus plant." He holds it up. "A simple cactus plant. The needles have been taken out and reversed so that they are pointing inside the plant instead of at you and me. After that, pebbles are added, and when the cactus dries the result is truly musical."

He turns it over again, and we all listen while the cafeteria fills with the sound of rain. And when he's sure we're all going to stay quiet, he puts it beneath the podium and says, "I carry it with me as a reminder that hidden in even the most echinate circumstance is the opportunity to produce something worthwhile, even lovely." He holds up his book and says, "Jimmy Slater at thirteen decided to take what little was given him and turn it into *opportunity*." Then he goes on to tell us how Jimmy Slater is this boy in his book who grew up on a farm in Kansas with a father who drank all the time, a mother who cried all the time, two little sisters and a broken-down tractor.

When Miss Pilson told us about her professor's book, I thought it was going to be the most boring assembly I'd ever been to. But the way Professor

Yates talked to us – it was like sitting around a campfire listening to stories. And when he read from his book, it wasn't like being in Miss Pilson's class listening to Old English. It was like being little again and having Grams read to me at bedtime. I liked it.

I wasn't thinking about Heather or Jared or Amber or what colour my shoes were. I was just listening. That is, until Marissa nudged me and pointed to her watch and I realized that there were only fifteen minutes left before the end of school. All of a sudden I forgot about Jimmy Slater and his farm, and my heart started pounding and my hands started sweating. I whispered, "You ready?"

I don't think Marissa had been paying much attention to Professor Yates because there wasn't much left of her thumbnail. She nods, so I say to Dot, "Remember, we'll meet you outside the front gate, right after school."

Marissa and I stand up and head for the back door. Marissa's got her arm around me, and I'm kind of doubled up with one hand over my mouth and the other over my stomach. At first I thought we were going to sail by all those teachers at the back door. But Mr Vince, who's the eighth-grade history teacher, stops us and says, "Where do you girls think you're going?"

I didn't say anything. I just held my stomach and

bugged my eyes out, looking kind of panicky. Then I started panting and smacking my lips, and Marissa says, "Mr Vince, she's going to be *sick*."

Well, he steps aside like he just noticed a dog turd on the sidewalk.

One of the teachers calls, "Need any help?"

Marissa says, "No, that's OK," and before you know it the cafeteria doors are closing and we're outside. All alone.

We hurried over to the side door of the office and took out two packs of ketchup that we'd saved from Marissa's lunch. I pulled up her sleeve and start squirting. Pretty soon we've got a little lake of ketchup on her arm, and when we pull her sleeve back down, ketchup seeps through the fibres, looking just like blood. We smile at each other and say, "Let's go!"

Now, I'd never been inside the office during an assembly. I'd always been *at* the assembly. So walking into the office while the rest of the school was locked up in the cafeteria was pretty strange. It was *quiet*. The door to the teachers' lounge was open for once, but there were no coffee cups, no teachers. Mr Caan's door was shut tight, and there were no kids waiting for him to yell at them. There were no people at the front counter or walking down the hall, either. Just as we'd hoped, the only

157

person around was the school secretary, Mrs Tweeter.

Mrs Tweeter gets up from behind her desk and says, "Why aren't you ladies at the assembly?" Then she sees Marissa's arm. "My dear, what *happened*?"

I give her a real serious look. "She tripped and smashed her arm into a chair and –" and that's all Mrs Tweeter needs to come swooping in for a closer look.

Marissa says, "It looks worse than it is. I just need a few bandages."

The closer Mrs Tweeter gets, the more worried I am that her nose is going to know that something's fishy. I pull Marissa back a little. "Mr Caan said a cold compress would be a good idea too. Do you have any ice?"

"A cold compress. Yes, yes, of course." She twirls around, going nowhere, then says, "Follow me down to First Aid."

I don't know if Marissa was acting, or if she was so scared she really *was* going to faint, but she puts her hand to her head and says, "I feel really lightheaded," and then kind of collapses into one of the lobby chairs.

Mrs Tweeter says, "Oh . . . oh, dear! OK. You stay right there. I'll be back before you know it."

I knew I didn't have much time, so before Mrs

Tweeter's even out the door I pull the tape recorder out of my pocket, flip over the counter, and head for the PA box.

And there I am with the school's public-address system at my fingertips and what do I do? I freeze. I can't move, I can't breathe, and I can't *think*. My brain feels like it's kissed an ice cube.

Marissa's up and out of the chair. She whispers, "What's the matter?"

"I don't know!" I can feel time ticking away, but there I am, acting like a bug in a glacier.

Then I remember Heather – Heather laughing at me, Heather telling stories about me, Heather making phone calls pretending to be me. And I start heating up. Way up. I punch the red button on the main panel and say, "May I have your attention! Please excuse the interruption. We have a very important announcement." Then I hit the play button on the tape recorder and let her rip.

When I hear Heather's voice come across the PA, my heart lets loose like fireworks. It's so *loud*. I can hear it echoing from outside, and there she is, larger than life, saying "Who does that stupid Sammy Keyes think she is? Telling me I've got egg breath. . ." and "I guess I'll just have to give Amber a little reason to beat her up *for* me." Then "Hi, Jared. This is Sammy. . ." and on and on about how much she loves him and would appreciate him and stuff. It's *embarrassing*.

The whole time Heather's voice is booming around campus the little part of my brain that's still working is wondering if any of this is getting into the cafeteria, and if it is, how long it's going to be before Mr Caan comes flying *out* of the cafeteria.

And it felt like an hour, but I knew the whole recording was only about two minutes long, so when Heather finally says, "Sammy Keyes, that'll teach you to call me Egg Breath," I click off the recorder and say into the PA, "The truth's out, Heather," and let go of the button.

I'm just swinging back over the counter when I hear the side door slam open and I know – that's not Mrs Tweeter back with first-aid supplies. It's Mr Caan, and he's seconds away from suspending us for life.

We go crashing out the front door, down the steps, and across the lawn, and we're barely through the gate when the dismissal bell rings.

Knowing Mr Caan, we figured he would chase us until he caught us. So we ran like crazy for a while and then dived into some bushes. And we're all scrunched up, with our eyes bugged out, panting and watching and waiting for Mr Caan's size fourteens to come stomping by, only they never do.

When enough time passes, we crawl out of the bushes and dust each other off. Then we see Dot, waving and shouting, "You did it! You did it!"

I slap her hand. "Could you understand it?"

"You could hear every *word*. When you said, 'May I have your attention,' all the teachers looked around like, 'What? What? Who's making the announcement? It must be an emergency!' And then when Heather started talking about egg breath, the whole place got so quiet you could hear the flies buzzing. And when Heather says that bit about appreciating Jared, Amber charges across the cafeteria at Heather and starts *wailing* on her. You wouldn't believe it! Perfect little Amber's screaming and pulling Heather's hair and scratching her face – it looked like she was going to kill her! And everybody's just standing there with their mouths open, *watching*, until Mr Tiller and Mr Pele break it up. Then Miss Pilson tries to get everyone to sit down, but of course it's too late – the whole school's gone crazy. Then the bell rings, and everyone just charges out of there." Dot laughs. "It was the best assembly I've ever been to. I can't believe you guys actually pulled it off!"

161

When we get done slapping each other's hands, Dot looks around and whispers, "What do you think they're going to *do* to you?"

"I don't know. Mr Caan'll probably throw me in the Box for a week." Then I laugh and say, "Maybe he'll expel me, who knows? I guess I'll find out tomorrow!" I turn to Marissa. "Remember: you didn't know what I was going to do. It was all my idea. Don't give yourself away, OK?"

She does a bit of the McKenze dance and nods.

We start walking, and before you know it we're at the mall, still talking about Heather and Amber and what it's going to be like the next day at school, and I'm nowhere *near* ready to go home. I'm supposed to, but a senior highrise is not exactly where you want to go right after you've paid back your worst enemy in spades.

So I just keep right on walking, and Marissa asks, "Are you heading over to Hudson's?"

"That's a great idea!"

Dot says, "Hey, can I come?" because she's heard a lot about him but she's never met him.

I laugh and say, "Sure."

When we get to Hudson's, he calls from the porch, "Good afternoon, ladies! What a pleasant surprise."

I introduce Dot to him, and then quicker than

she can quit whispering about his red suede boots, Hudson's back with iced tea and crackers. "You girls are sparkling like a disco ball. I take it your research got the results you were hoping for, Sammy."

That got us giggling, and pretty soon Hudson can't stand it any more. "Tell me what you did!"

I pull out his recorder and hand it over. "Thanks for the loan, Hudson."

Hudson Graham doesn't need an instruction manual to figure out what he's supposed to do. He presses PLAY, and when Heather's voice starts filling up his porch he kicks those red boots of his up on to the railing and listens. And by the time there's nothing left but static, he's laughing so hard he almost falls out of his chair. "So, who'd you play this for?"

I grin and say, "The whole school."

He looks puzzled. "How?"

We all say, "Over the PA!"

Dot adds, "During an *assembly*. It was the greatest!" Then she tells him all about Heather and Amber scratching and clawing and tearing each other up.

When Dot's done, Hudson shakes his head and says, "Unbelievable." He raises his tea and we all clink glasses. "To research well done. Congratulations!"

We're all in the middle of taking our sips when the phone rings. And rings and rings and rings. And at first Hudson waves it off, but after it rings some more he gets up and answers it.

When he comes back he says, "Sammy, it's your grandmother. She sounds rather upset."

So I go inside, and the first thing Grams says is, "Samantha, *why*? How could you get yourself in this much trouble? Mr Caan's calling a parent conference! What am I supposed to do about a parent conference?"

"Did you tell him Mom was visiting Aunt Valerie?"

She snaps, "It's *Victoria*, and, yes, that's what I told him, but I can't keep this up for ever! And now he's expecting *me* to attend this meeting." She takes a deep breath. "I know this has something to do with Heather because Mr Caan said that she and her mother will be at the conference tomorrow, but, good Lord, Samantha, he made it sound like you held the entire school hostage! What on earth did you do?"

Well, I'm not about to explain it to her over the phone. I've tried that before, and it just doesn't work. "Grams, please. Calm down, OK? I'll be right home and explain the whole thing."

So I said bye to everyone and headed home as

fast as I could. And as I hurried down Cypress it started sinking in: Maybe I'd stopped Heather from making me look like a complete idiot over Jared, but now I had a whole new set of problems – bigger than the last.

And I wasn't ready to jump on another runaway train; I'd just survived the last one. So when I saw Bargain Books and remembered Grams' book, I thought that bringing it home might distract her from scolding me about what I'd done at school. At least cut it short.

So I ran across Broadway and into Bargain Books thinking it would only take a minute to get the thing.

Boy, was I wrong.

Fifteen

Mr Bell was in the middle of buying books. His hair was sticking out even more than usual, and he didn't even say hello when I walked in. He just kept digging through a big box that a man had brought in, putting the books in three different stacks, kind of frowning with one side of his mouth and smiling with the other.

The guy who was selling the books wasn't exactly the kind of person who mowed his own yard, if you know what I mean. He had on white slacks and a pinkie ring, which tells you something right there, but it was his feet that made me keep my distance. See, he was wearing loafers. Loafers with no socks.

He's got his eye on Mr Bell like he's dealing poker instead of stacking books, and if you were just watching him from the knees up, you'd think Pinkie Ring was just making sure that Mr Bell was doing his job right. But Pinkie's toes are popping around inside his loafers like little mice trying to get out of a paper bag. And the more I stand there watching those toes trying to come up for air, the more I wonder what this guy's so anxious about.

When Mr Bell gets to the bottom of the box, he pushes one stack towards Pinkie and says, "I can't take these." Then he points to the other stacks and says, "I'll give you twenty for this group and a fourth the cover price for these."

Pinkie's eyebrow barely goes up, but his toes practically pop through his shoes. "*What*? Twenty for all of these?" He picks a book off the top of the third stack. "And you're telling me you'll only give me two fifty for this? It's barely used! It may never even have been read! That's highway robbery!"

Mr Bell takes a deep breath and pushes up a sleeve. "I can give you thirty per cent, but that would be store credit."

"You mean I gotta turn around and spend my money here?"

Mr Bell nods and points to a sign by the cash register. "It's our policy. Twenty-five per cent cash, thirty per cent store credit. You can take them elsewhere if you'd like."

Pinkie's toes are working up quite a sweat. He mumbles, "You're the only game in town, and you know it. Gimme the cash."

Mr Bell takes out a calculator, but before he starts punching in numbers I say, "Mr Bell? I'm sorry to interrupt. I was just hoping my grandmother's book came in?"

He blinks at me like he didn't realize I was there. "It has, Sammy. Let me finish up here, OK? I'll only be a minute."

I stand back, waiting and wondering why Pinkie's so uptight about getting rid of a few old books, when the back of my brain starts twitching a little. And while Mr Bell's counting out Pinkie's money, I go up to the stacks of books and start reading the titles. And it doesn't take a genius to figure that these are not books Mr Pinkie Ring would be reading himself. There are romance books and gardening books and a ton of books on *doll* collecting.

Pinkie's toes finally get their way. He's out the door and down the street before his wallet's even back in his hip pocket.

I say, "He sure seemed nervous."

Mr Bell rolls his eyes. "Customers like that I can do without."

"These don't seem like books he would read."

"That they don't."

For a second there everything seemed to be in slow motion. The ceiling fan, the register closing – the whole place felt like a dream. "What if they were *stolen*?"

Mr Bell laughs. "Then he went through a lot of trouble for nothing! There's no money in used books."

He pulls out Grams' book from behind the counter and says, "So what kind of business is your grandmother thinking about starting?"

At first I don't know what he's talking about. Then I notice the title of the book she'd ordered: *Establishing a Mail Order Business*. "I don't know!"

I must have looked shocked, because Mr Bell laughs and says, "People are full of little surprises, aren't they?"

I laugh and say, "You've got that right!" and head out the door and across the street. And I've pounded up two and a half flights of fire escape stairs when I feel this thought kind of chasing behind me. And when I get to the third-floor landing, it tackles me – boom!

When I can move again, I don't keep heading up the stairs. I do a U-turn and pound back down. And when I'm at the bottom, I take Grams' book, stuff it in my backpack, and tuck the pack behind some bushes along the building. Then I start running. And I keep right on running until I'm at Chauncy's doorstep.

I don't try any of the SOS stuff – I just start pounding. Pounding and yelling, "Chauncy! Answer the door! I've got to ask you something! Chauncy! Hey, Chauncy! I'm not going away! Answer the door!" Finally he does.

I'm expecting him to look mad or irritated or impatient or *something*, but all he looks is tired. Real tired. Like he's been up for three days without any sleep. And when I ask, "Can I come in?" he just sighs and nods and leads me down the hall.

He sits down in the chair I found him in on Halloween, looking just about as alive as he had that night, and points to the chair next to him.

Well, sitting's about the *last* thing I want to do. I've got all this blood pumping through me from running, but on top of that, I can't stop moving because the more I think about what I want to ask him, the more I'm sure that I don't *have* to ask him. I'm right.

I walk around looking back and forth from him to the bookcases. "Chauncy, do you own any rare and valuable books?"

He studies me a minute, then nods.

I come in a few steps. "Are you missing any?"

He gives me a puzzled look, but then shakes his head.

"Are you *sure*?"

He sits up a bit and turns sideways to look at a bookcase with glass doors. Then he faces me again and says, "I'm . . . sure."

I go racing over to the bookcase and, sure

170

enough, it's packed. I open the doors and after a minute I say, "Chauncy! Come here." And while he's walking over I read out, *"Secrets of Southern Cooking, Revisiting Vietnam, The Candy Cane Chronicles...* These may look old, but they sure don't look too valuable!"

Chauncy LeBard doesn't have much colour in his cheeks to begin with, so when I turn to look at him staring at his bookcase, what I see is a ghost. He says "No!" and before you know it he's pawing through the books, pulling out the ones I found plus two more. When he's done he stands there shaking. "They're ... gone!"

I sit him down because he looks like he's about to faint. "Who knew you had them, and how much were they worth?"

He sits there a minute and then gets his buzz box. "I don't know who knew. They've been in the family for years. They were my mother's pride and joy! I never even thought –" All of a sudden he starts crying, and I can barely understand him when he says, "I should've put them in a safe-deposit box."

I didn't know what to do, so I kind of stood there like an idiot watching him cry. Finally I put my hand on his shoulder and ask, "Were they worth a lot?"

He wipes his eyes and nods.

"A thousand? Five thousand?"

He kind of shudders. "Closer to a hundred. Maybe one fifty."

"Thousand?"

Sure enough, he nods.

Then I remember that Douglas LeBard cut off his wife when she mentioned an appraiser. "Were they appraised after your mother died?"

"Right before."

"Do you know the names of the books?"

He closes his eyes and puts a hand on his forehead. "There was a *Tales* by Poe. . ."

I jump up and get a pen and some paper. "Wait, wait, wait. . . OK, *Tales* by Poe?"

"Yes, there were two by Edgar Allan Poe. *Tales* and *Al Aaraaf, Tamerlane and Minor Poems.*"

I write this down as best I can. "What did they look like?"

"*Tales* had buff wraps, and the other had blue boards."

"Wait a minute. Wraps? Boards? What are those?"

"Wraps are dust jackets; boards are the hard cover of a book."

I let this sink in and then say, "So one had a kind of skin-coloured cover, and the other was a blue book?"

He shrugs and nods as if to say, *Close enough.*

I write this all down and ask, "OK, what else?"

"There was a Darwin – *On the Origin of Species by Means of Natural Selection. . .*"

I sit up and say, "*Charles* Darwin?" because that's all we've heard about for weeks in science.

He gives me a twitch of a smile. "Yes. It's green cloth and a first London edition. There was also a copy of Hemingway's first book, *Three Stories and Ten Poems*, and *The Celebrated Jumping Frog of Calaveras County and Other Sketches* by Mark Twain. That one's plum-coloured, with a frog in the left corner of the cover."

I don't need to ask him "*Ernest* Hemingway?" because Miss Pilson's dissected his stories for us in class and found hidden meanings where you know Ernest had never meant to hide anything. And since everyone's heard of Mark Twain, all I said was, "Anything else?"

He thinks a minute and then shakes his head. "How did you know?"

So I tell him about the lady in red high heels who bought two big boxes of old-looking books from Bargain Books and what Mr Bell had said about one old book looking like another.

"I could ask Mr Bell if anyone has come in trying to sell some rare books."

Chauncy shakes his head. "They wouldn't go through Tommy. They're too valuable."

We stand around a minute, and then I say, "I think I ought to get the police to come over, don't you?"

He sighs and nods.

"It's on my way home. I'll give them this list and tell them to come over, OK?"

So off I go, and I'm thinking that the first thing I'm going to do is call Grams from the station and let her know that I'm all right. Trouble is, I never got that far.

Where I got to was the end of Orange Street. Orange Street tees into Miller, and you can either walk a mile down Miller Street to a crosswalk, or half a block *up* Miller Street to the crosswalk at Cook. Of course, if you're in a *car* you can also go straight, which will take you right up the driveway of the courthouse. But if you're a pedestrian, that choice is illegal – it's called jaywalking.

I jaywalked all right, only it was more like jay*running*, because Miller's a pretty busy street. And I had just about made it over to the other side when a police car comes squealing out of the courthouse parking lot with its siren going and its lights flashing. It does a U-turn right in the middle of all this traffic on Miller, then comes bouncing up the handicapped ramp across the sidewalk and nosedives to a stop right in front of me.

Well, you'd better believe I thought something serious was going down. Until I saw that the driver was my hero Officer Borsch. That's right, Santa Martina's finest was wailing and flashing and tearing up the courthouse lawn so he could write the town's most renowned jaywalker a ticket.

He gets out of his car with his pad and his pen ready, looking like a pit bull that's just chewed through its leash, but before he can say anything, I go up to the passenger window and knock on it until Muscles rolls it down. Now you can tell that Muscles is not too happy about being parked on the courthouse lawn, but he shakes his head and says, "You need to work this out with him."

I say, "I jaywalked because I was in a hurry to tell you what I discovered at Chauncy LeBard's. Look at this. It's a list of books that were stolen from him on Halloween. They're what the Skeleton Man was after."

"Some *books*?"

"They're worth a hundred thousand dollars!"

Officer Borsch snaps, "What the devil are you doing, Keith? I've got a citation to write!"

Muscles flexes himself out of the car. "Hang on a minute, Gil. She's discovered some important evidence in that Bush House break-in. There are some books missing. She says they're—"

Officer Borsch rolls his eyes. "Oh, give me a break! It's *books*, now? I've got more important things to do than listen to this."

I couldn't quite believe my ears when Muscles mumbles, "Yeah, like writing jaywalking citations."

I guess Officer Borsch couldn't quite believe his ears either, because he takes a step closer to Muscles, sticks his stomach out even further than it already is, and says, "What?"

Muscles throws his hands up in the air. "What's *with* you, Gil? You act like this girl's been spraying graffiti instead of trying to help us with this Bush House thing. You said yourself our Q and A with the brother was enlightening. *She's* the one that gave us the idea, remember?"

Blood's rising like a tide in Officer Borsch's face. He takes a step closer and gives Muscles a quick two-handed shove on the chest. "You listen here, you overpumped pipsqueak—"

Muscles shoves him right back. "No, *you* listen, you bloated dinosaur. The books that got ripped off are worth over a hundred *thousand* dollars..." He looks at me like, *Is that right?* so I nod up and down real fast. He turns back to Borsch and yells, "You hear me? A hundred thousand dollars! You were looking for a motive. *There's* your motive, bucko!"

The whole time Muscles is yelling at him Officer

Borsch is getting redder and redder, and sweat's starting to bead up on his forehead. He yells back, "You've got a lot to learn about being a cop, buddy! I don't know how a guy like you even got on the force!" While he's yelling, he's poking Muscles in the chest with his pudgy finger, and Muscles is standing there taking it, but you can tell that it won't be long before Muscles decks him.

I jump in between them and say, "Hey! Hey, look what you guys are doing. You're gonna cause an accident!" because traffic is stopped in both directions on both streets.

Muscles and Officer Borsch stare each other down for a minute, and then Officer Borsch gets back in the squad car. And after he's backed out into traffic, Muscles sighs and says, "I'd like to hear the rest of the story, if you don't mind." He leads me into the courtyard of the courthouse, and I sit on a bench and tell him all about how someone had replaced Chauncy's most valuable books with some random old books so that no one would know at a glance that anything was missing. Then, when I tell him how Douglas LeBard had interrupted his wife when she had said something about an appraiser, and that the books had been in the family for a long, long time, Muscles says, "Sounds like something the brother might want to get his hands on for more than one reason."

"Exactly."

He stands up and says, "I'm going to head over to LeBard's and get a report, then I'll see if I can't get a search warrant issued for the brother's residence tonight." He shakes my hand and says, "I'm sorry you had to witness that . . . that *scene*. It's been building up since they teamed us together." He scratches the back of his neck. "I don't know what it is – Gil took a dislike to me the first time he laid eyes on me."

I laugh and say, "I know the feeling!"

We say goodbye, and he jaywalks across Orange, and I head off to jaywalk across Cook.

For a while I'm caught up thinking about Officer Borsch ignoring so many traffic laws so he could write me up for jaywalking. But by the time I reach Maynard's Market, this new little twitch in the back of my brain is snapping around louder and louder, until finally I have to admit that this whole Skeleton Man business still doesn't make any sense. I mean, if it *is* Chauncy's brother, why did he get rid of the candlesticks? They had sentimental value, too. And why would he rob his brother if he was trying to kill him? If he killed him he would get the inheritance, and he wouldn't have to rob him. And if he *robbed* him, he'd have what he wanted and he wouldn't have to kill him.

And the more I think about it, the more I understand that I'm going down the right river.

I'm just on the wrong boat.

Sixteen

It was already too late *not* to be in trouble, but I was hurrying anyway. Instead of going clear around back to the fire escape, I decided to risk it and go in the front lobby and use the elevator. And I might have been able to sneak by Mr Garnucci, but as I'm coming in, the elevator doors open, and guess who's coming out? Mrs Graybill. And under this fuzzy white sweater she's wearing her honeysuckle hurricane, and on top of her head she's got neat little curls, like she's spent all day at the hairdresser. I duck behind this plastic tree that's collecting dust in the corner, and watch as a man follows her off the elevator. He's not anybody I've seen around the building before. He's *old* all right, but he looks more like he's spent his life on the putting green than in a highrise apartment. He's wearing white shoes, white pants and a white polo shirt, and everything else about him is tanned.

Mr Garnucci calls over from an easy chair, "Don't you two look splendid! Have a nice evening, Daisy." He winks and adds, "You take good care of her, Mr Belmont!"

Mr Belmont clicks his dentures into place. "You can count on that, sir."

Mrs Graybill waves and calls, "Good night, Vince," and off they go.

So I'm standing there behind this dusty plastic tree, and the coast is clear for me to zip up the elevator and explain everything to Grams. But I can't move. My brain is working so hard that my legs can't work at all. And the longer I stand there thinking, the more covered I get with goosebumps, until finally I just slide down the wall and sit in the corner and stare.

Who knows how long I was there. All I know is that when my legs started working again, they didn't take me up the elevator. They took me straight out the front door and across the street to Bargain Books.

I didn't know what I was going to do if I was right. I didn't think that far ahead. It was a crazy idea, but it made sense. And if I *was* right, there probably wasn't much time left to get proof.

When I got to Bargain Books, I squatted against the wall outside the door and closed my eyes. Tight. And I left them closed for what felt like an hour. Then I took a deep breath, stumbled to the door, and squeezed in. Once I was inside, I didn't have to stand around waiting for my eyes to adjust, because right away I could see.

Mr Bell's up in the loft helping a customer, so I tiptoe over to his platform, swing open the gate and sneak behind the register to his desk. There are stacks of books and mountains of papers and all kinds of boxes – on his desk, around his desk, everywhere.

Part of me's panicking because it can't come up with a good excuse for being where I definitely don't belong, but the other part keeps one eye on the loft and starts poking around. I check inside boxes and behind boxes and all around his desk but I don't find anything. Then I think to go *through* the desk. So I tug on the bottom drawer, but it's locked.

This is a pretty old desk – really deep and sturdy-looking – but the keyhole of the centre drawer is loose and looks like you could just snap it off. So I'm looking around for something to pry down the lock, but just as I'm reaching over to snag the butter knife that's lying across a jar of raspberry jam, I hear the steps of the loft squeaking and creaking. Mr Bell says to the customer, ". . .that's the only other author that I can think of. You might want to give Higuera Books in Santa Luisa a call. They may have a few titles by him."

I take a quick look around, but it's too late to make it off the platform before I get noticed. So I squeeze in between all this junk that's under the desk, pull in the chair and scrunch back as far as I can.

A few seconds later Tommy Bell comes through the gate. And while he's ringing up his customer I'm holding my breath, trying to scan through the junk under the desk for something to cover me up. There's a roll of paper towels on top of an old pair of shoes. There's a box of printer paper with the lid half off, and behind it I see what looks like the corner of a sheet. So very slowly I reach over and pull the sheet from behind the box, but what I wind up holding is a pillowcase.

A green-and-white striped pillowcase.

All of a sudden I can't seem to breathe right, and my whole body's got the shivers. And I'm wondering, what was I *thinking*, coming here by myself?

After the customer leaves, I can hear Mr Bell shuffling some papers, and then here come his feet, right by the chair. He goes over to the table against the wall and pops an English muffin in his toaster. His shiny, brand-new toaster.

As his muffins are heating up, he mixes himself a cup of coffee, and I'm thinking *I'm* toast! I mean, there's no way a man who'd knock someone out for some old books would find me under his desk and tell me to just run along. No way.

As I'm sitting there shivering under the Skeleton Man's desk, it hits me that what's between me and Chauncy's books is probably only two centimetres of wood. Two centimetres of really hard, old wood. Just then I hear Mr Bell say, "May I help you?" and there go his shoes across the platform.

So I'm all by myself again. But I know it won't be for long, because on the table are two English muffins covered with raspberry jam.

I thought about staying there, scrunched up under the desk all night. But even as I was thinking that would be the smart thing to do, my hand was out, snagging that butter knife. And the next thing you know, I've got one eye on the lookout for Mr Bell, and the other watching my hands wiggle and pry and mangle the lock. And just when I thought the lock was never going to give, *snap!* it broke.

The snap sounded like a shot to me, but I figured it was now or never, so very carefully I tugged open the first drawer.

And what's in it? Nothing. Just a bunch of folders and papers and stuff. I close it and open the next drawer, and what's in that one? Calculators and marking pens and printer ribbons – not one book. By now I'm sweating, and my heart's about pounding out of my body, but when I open the bottom drawer, there waiting to hop into my lap is a frog. A frog on a plum-coloured book. And underneath *The Celebrated Jumping Frog of Calaveras County* is *Three Stories and Ten Poems*, and underneath *that* are the other three books.

I get them out of the drawer as fast as I can, and when I look around for something to put them in, there's that pillowcase just waiting for me. So I hurry to stuff the books in, but I'm not fast enough. One minute I'm by myself; the next minute Mr Bell is stepping on to the platform.

He knows right off that I'm not there to snag his muffins. He comes charging at me saying, "Why, you little. . ."

Running through my mind is a picture of Chauncy all slumped over and dripping blood. And there's no way I want to wind up like *that*, but I'm stuck on the platform and I don't see how I'm going to get away.

Then I realize that in my hand is a pillowcase full of books – your basic hundred-thousand-dollar weapon. And when Bones gets near me I wind it around my hand and swing with all my might.

I connect, but barely. And it doesn't really slow him down. He comes at me again, his shirt cuffs dangling and his wild hair sticking out, and in his eyes I see panic. Sheer panic – like a man grabbing

185

on to weeds as he's falling off a cliff. And I realize that this man will do anything for these books – *anything*.

And I'm backing up, running out of room, scrambling around for some way out, when I decide that I have to try again. I wind up the pillowcase and this time I swing it clear around, and *wham!* I hit him right in the temple.

I wasn't expecting him to go down, but down he went. And as he's lying there looking pretty knocked out, I reach for the phone to call 911. But just as I get to the phone, he starts getting up.

I punch in 911, but I don't have a chance to say a word. Mr Bell grabs me by the leg, and the phone goes flying, and all of a sudden I'm down on the floor right next to him.

The pillowcase is still wrapped around my hand, but I'm not in a position to use it. He's got one hand clamped around my leg and the other yanking on the books, and the look in his eye is telling me that any minute he's going to drop both so he can bash my head against the wall.

I'm kicking him like mad, trying to break free, and as I'm looking around for something to help me out, I notice the toaster right above me. I let go of the pillowcase, pull the plug out of the

186

socket, and with both hands I reach up and yank the toaster free. Then, *blamo!* I slam it on his head.

For a second there, he collapsed. And I thought he was knocked out for good, but before I can get back to the phone he starts to groan and move around a bit.

So I'm looking around for a way to *keep* him down, when I get an idea. I sit on his back, hard, then pull his hands together and wrap them up with the cord of the toaster.

He groans and his hands start twitching, and I can tell – he's coming round. So I put his hands in the slots of the toaster and push down the lever. Then I pull the end of the cord to the wall socket and say, "Mr Bell, if you make one little move that I don't like I'm going to have to toast you."

He starts to roll over, so I plug the thing in. Just for a second.

He yelps, and his eyes open wide, and he whispers, "You're crazy."

I just stay there with the plug poised near the socket. "I'm serious."

He lies there for a second, looking at me, and then all of a sudden his head flops down and he starts crying. And pretty soon he's sobbing like a baby, so I drag the phone over with my foot and say, "Hello?"

The emergency lady says, "I'm right here. Are you all right?"

"I could use some help."

"It's on the way. Actually, they should already be there."

The way my luck with the police department had been running I was expecting his Royal Rudeness to come cruising through the door, so I was pretty relieved when two policemen I'd never seen before came barging in.

I call, "Back here!"

They come swinging through the gate and whip off their sunglasses. Then they just stand there, looking at Mr Bell lying on the floor with his hands in a toaster.

They ask me what's going on, but I can't tell them that I'm about to toast this guy because he stole some books from a man with no voice – it just wouldn't translate right. So I try starting at the top, but telling about being ploughed over by a skeleton, stomping out a fire and finding Frankenstein tied to a chair isn't making things clear either. About halfway through, one of them puts up a hand and says, "Whoa, whoa, whoa!"

So I sigh and do something I never imagined I'd

do. "Could you just call Officer Borsch or his partner and tell them we've caught the Skeleton Man?"

The next thing you know they're filling the room with static, ten-fouring and ten-nining into their walkie-talkies. Finally one of them says, "Officer Emerson'll be right over," and then goes about reading Mr Bell his rights.

When Muscles comes flexing through the door, he's waving a paper in his hand. He laughs and says, "You're telling me I cashed in all my favours for a search warrant I don't need?"

I kind of laugh too. "Sorry."

He takes one look at Mr Bell, handcuffed and looking kind of small in a chair against the wall. "*That's* him?"

I say, "That's him. I haven't found the skeleton suit, but I found the pillowcase, and I found these in his desk." I hand the books to him, and after a minute of looking them over he says, "*These* are worth a hundred thousand dollars?"

"That's right."

They all kind of gawk at them, then Muscles says, "So what happened since I saw you at the courthouse? I thought you thought it was the brother."

So I tell him that the candlesticks winding up at the Thrift Store bothered me – how it didn't make any sense for Chauncy's brother to throw away something with a lot of sentimental value. And then I tell him how Mr Bell had said that he was looking for a buyer for his store and how when I mentioned Chauncy he acted like he didn't even *know* him.

Then I start telling him how Mrs Graybill and Mr Belmont were talking to Mr Garnucci and how Mr Garnucci called Mr Belmont "Mr Belmont" because he didn't really know him, and how he called Mrs Graybill "Daisy" 'cause he *did* know her. And I'm just warming up to the point of all this when Muscles shakes his head and says, "Sammy, you're losing me again."

I take a deep breath and say, "When I was at Chauncy's today and we found out about the books, I offered to ask Mr Bell if anyone had tried to sell him some rare books. And Chauncy said, 'They wouldn't go through *Tommy*,' like he knew him. At the time I didn't think about it, but after I heard Mr Garnucci talking in the lobby, well, it all clicked.

"I think that Mr Bell is the one who appraised Chauncy's books and that he's been dying to get his hands on them ever since. Chauncy could tell you for sure. So could his brother."

Mr Bell is sitting with his hands handcuffed in

his lap, and he's crying. He looks up at me and says, "Sammy, I'm *so* sorry. I never meant to hurt you. Or Chauncy. Things just got out of hand. I couldn't stop thinking about them! And then the nightmares started. That place going up in smoke . . . those books, wasted. Gone for ever. . ." He puts his head in his hands and starts bawling. "Why couldn't they have been mine?"

One of the police officers puts a hand on his shoulder and says, "Come along, Mr Bell. It's over."

So they take him away, leaving me with Muscles to answer a bunch of questions for his report.

When Muscles finishes writing everything down, he walks me to the kerb and shakes my hand. And as he's pumping away, saying thanks for all the help, this guy pops out of nowhere and takes our picture. We're both kind of stunned, wondering what's going on, when the photographer puts down his camera and says, "Joseph Jennings, *Santa Martina Times*. We understand there's been an arrest made here tonight. It was Thomas Bell, the bookstore owner – is that correct?"

Before I can say a thing, Muscles puts one of his iron arms up and says, "I'm sorry, we're not at liberty to answer any questions at this time." Then he says to me, "You need a ride home?"

I just laugh and say, "No, thanks," because getting a ride from him would take a whole lot longer than jaywalking.

So I wave goodbye and cut across the street. I suddenly remember that I stashed my backpack and as I'm digging it out of the bushes I'm thinking that I'll probably be up all night explaining everything to Grams.

And normally that would have been fine. It's just that the next day was going to be a big day at school.

A really big day.

Seventeen

Grams forgave me around midnight. Then she wanted to spend the next hour talking about what *not* to say at Mr Caan's meeting the next day. And after she went to bed I still had to do my maths homework, so it felt like I'd slept for all of ten seconds when the alarm clock went off.

While I'm in the shower trying to jump-start myself, Grams is in the kitchen making oatmeal and talking to someone on the phone. And when I get done inhaling my breakfast, Grams puts on her coat and says, "Hudson's on his way over to give us a ride. He's probably already waiting."

A ride. What a relief! I throw my backpack on my shoulder and say, "I'll meet you out front." Then I run down the fire escape, around the building and over to the parking lot where Hudson is just pulling up in Jester.

The whole way to school Hudson kept asking me questions about Tommy Bell and the books, and by the time we pulled into the school parking lot he was saying, "I think it's about time I paid Chauncy LeBard a visit. This recluse business has gone on far too long." He turns to Grams. "I'll be right here when you get done." Then he says to me, "Any chance you'll be coming home with us?"

I grin and say, "Oh, there's a *big* chance of that, but if my plan comes off it'll be just you and Grams."

Grams is halfway out of the car, but when she hears that she stops cold. "*What* plan? We didn't discuss any plan!"

"Grams, don't *worry*. It's nothing bad. I just hope it works."

She gets out of the car, and I can see her shaking her head at Hudson, but he says, "Just relax, Rita. The meeting will be over before you know it."

So off we go, up the steps, in the front door, past Mrs Tweeter and straight to Mr Caan's office. And right there in the hallway are Heather and her mother, waiting.

Mrs Acosta's outfit is a little more conservative than the one she was wearing at the Halloween party. At least, I think *she* thinks so. She's got on white high heels, a purple mini skirt, a fluffy white blouse and only three bracelets.

And we're all standing in the hallway pretending like we're not looking at each other, when Mr Caan comes over and ushers us to a meeting room with a table and some padded folding chairs. He says, "I think we'll be more comfortable in here," and then motions for us to have a seat.

Grams and I sit on one side of the table, and Heather and her mother sit on the other, and we're all kind of staring at our hands folded nice-and-neat in our laps. Mr Caan sits at the head of the table and says, "I'd like to begin by thanking you for coming." He clears his throat. "I realize there is a history of tension between these two young ladies, and I feel it's time we dialogued about the root of the problem so that maybe we can eradicate it once and for all. To start with, though, I'd like to address yesterday's events." He looks at me. "Now then, Samantha. I understand your frustration over the rumours about you and Jared. However, do you agree that using the school's public-address system to settle the score with Heather was entirely inappropriate?"

Before I can put together a nice way of not lying, I blurt out, "What would *you* have done if you were in my shoes, Mr Caan?"

Heather snickers, which makes Mr Caan turn to her and say, "You find that humorous, Heather?"

"I'm sorry, sir. I just can't see you in a pair of green high-tops."

Mrs Acosta elbows her and whispers, "Heather!"

Heather just shrugs. "Well, I *can't*."

Mr Caan takes a deep breath and then says to me, "What *I* would've done in your position is talk to one of my teachers or a counsellor or even an administrator. What I would *not* have done is taken it upon myself to hold the entire school hostage to my revenge!"

I look down and say real quietly, "Mr Caan, if I'd thought of another way to prove she was lying I would've done it. But you've got to understand – Heather is not *rational*. She gets mad over *nothing*, and she's got this way of getting the popular kids to believe her. How can I compete with that? What am I supposed to do? Run around to all the kids at school and say, 'Hey, listen to this! This is proof that I haven't been calling Jared – Heather has'? Like they'd believe me. And you can't reason with Heather. She gets so mad over stuff and, really, I never know what's going to set her off next."

I'm keeping my voice low and steady and mostly staring at my lap, but I'm keeping an eye on Heather, too. When I get to the part about her getting mad over nothing, she starts to say something, but her mother puts a hand on her shoulder and stops her. And I can tell that she can't wait for her turn to say some pretty choice things about *me*, so I finish by taking a deep breath and looking straight at her when I say, "I'm sorry to say this, but I really think Heather needs professional help."

Her mom jumps up. *"What?* How *dare* you! If anyone around here needs a psychiatrist, it's you! The lies you make up, the embarrassment you've put my daughter through! This is beyond belief!"

I give Grams a secret little wink, but she's looking pretty worried.

Mr Caan stands up. "Now, calm down, Mrs Acosta. We need to get to the bottom of this, and I think we're off to a good start." When Heather's mom sits down, he says, "OK now, Heather, what do you have to say in response to Samantha's observations?"

Heather bats her eyes at Mr Caan and sniffles, "She's just a mean, mean person. I don't do *anything* to deserve being treated the way she treats me. That tape . . . it was just something she faked. Can you believe anyone would *do* something like that?"

Now as she's trying to come up with some tears to make her lies a little more convincing, I'm pulling a pair of earrings out of my sweatshirt pocket. A pair of rubber ring earrings with fake rubies on them. And as Heather's whining away I very slowly reach up and clip one to my left ear. Then I clear my throat just a little so Heather'll glance over at me. And when she does, I give her a little smile and clip the other earring to my right ear.

For a second she just stares. Then she chokes out, "Where did you get those?"

I shake my head back and forth so the earrings dangle a bit. "At a party. I told the hostess they were the coolest earrings I'd ever seen, so she gave them to me."

Heather starts breathing real hard through her nose, and you can just see her thinking, *It can't be...It* can't *be!* So I give her a little smile and say, "They didn't exactly go with my princess costume, but it was real nice of her anyway."

That does it. Heather lets out a screech and comes clawing across the table at me. And before anyone can stop her she's on top of me screaming, "I hate you! I hate you! *I hate you!*"

I fall backward and call, "Help! Mr Caan, help! There she goes again! She's crazy! Somebody, please! Help me!"

Mrs Acosta yells, "Heather, stop it! Stop it! What's got *into* you? Heather!"

Before Heather can gouge me up too badly, Mr Caan pulls her off me and holds her arms behind her back. But does that stop her? No way. She kicks and screams, "I'm going to get you for this! I hate you! *I hate you!*"

Mr Caan yells at Mrs Acosta, "Follow me!" and then hauls Heather out of the room.

Twenty minutes later he finally comes back. He sits down and says with a big sigh, "Her mother's taken her home."

Grams gives him a prim look. "I do hope you'll have her seek some professional help. You can't have that kind of behaviour in a learning institution, for heaven's sake." Then she says, "Do you understand now what kind of stress Samantha has been under? What with the way that girl taunts her and teases her and got the whole school believing Samantha was calling that boy?"

Mr Caan puts up his hands. "I can understand why Samantha did what she did, but there still has to be some disciplinary action for her use of the PA system." He looks at me and says, "My inclination yesterday was to suspend you." He chuckles. "Indefinitely." He takes a deep breath and says, "In the light of what's just transpired, I'm not going to do *that*, but a detention is going to have to be assigned." He straightens his watch a bit and then looks me in the eye. "Last night I added up the hours you should serve for your various infractions, and it came to twenty. Twenty."

Grams says, "Mr Caan ... really!"

Mr Caan puts up a hand. "Twenty hours of after-school detention does seem a bit extreme, considering the circumstances, so what do you say we have Samantha put those twenty hours to better use – maybe doing a community service of some sort?"

I'm still stunned, thinking *Twenty hours!* but Grams is right on top of things. "St Mary's Church is always looking for volunteers this time of year to help with the Thanksgiving food drive. We could have her help out at the church and get Father Mayhew to verify her hours for you."

Mr Caan thinks about that for all of two seconds. "Great idea." He looks at me and says, "And now I think you should be getting to class, young lady. You've missed enough school as it is."

So I jump up, give Grams a kiss on the cheek, and off I go. And I could probably have just skipped English altogether since there were less than ten minutes left of the class, but I didn't want to push my luck. I tried just sneaking in, but Miss Pilson turned around from writing on the board just as I was scooting into my seat.

She stares at me like she's seeing a ghost. Then she blows up at her fringe and finishes assigning an essay for homework. When the bell rings and everyone else goes charging for the door, she says, "Samantha! A word, please," which, translated, means she's going to use a lot of big words to tell me how mad she is at me.

I go up to her, but before she can get a good string of adjectives together I say, "Miss Pilson, I'm sorry that I interrupted your assembly. I really liked Mr Yates, and I was *into* hearing about his book." I let out a sigh and say, "I know his coming to the school was a big deal for you. I'm *sorry*."

She stares at me a minute and kind of moves her lips from one side of her face to the other like she's got words in there trying to punch their way out. Finally she says, "Do you realize the mayhem you caused? It was complete chaos in there! I was mortified!" Then she sighs and says, "Martin Yates is not the kind of man who likes to be upstaged, Samantha. I doubt he'll ever agree to give another talk at *this* school."

I shuffle around a bit. "I really am sorry, Miss Pilson."

As I'm leaving she says, "Samantha? Why would Heather *do* such a thing?"

I shrug. "I guess she doesn't like the colour of my shoes."

She looks at me like she doesn't quite understand, but I leave anyway, knowing that she'll figure it out – after all, she's an English teacher.

I slip into maths class as the tardy bell's ringing, and right away I know something's up. In Mr Tiller's class you're in your seat with your pencil sharpened and your homework out *before* the bell's done ringing or you're in trouble. But as I'm sliding into my seat I see half the class waiting in line at the pencil sharpener, and the other half in their seats, stretching their necks around the people in front of them.

All I can see is Mr Tiller up there erasing the board. So I stretch my neck clear around Henry Regulski, who sits in front of me, but before I can see anything Henry whips his curly head around and says, "Check it out! I don't believe it."

"Believe *what*?"

Mr Tiller turns around and taps on the podium for us to settle down. And looking at him, everything seems pretty normal to me. He's got on a polo shirt, some random slacks with a little chalk dust on them here and there, and . . . and . . . green high-tops!

He gives me a quick grin and a wink and calls, "Hey, you clowns, settle down! We've got a lot to cover today. Pass your homework left. Let's go!"

For the rest of class it was *quiet* in there. Nobody asked about the shoes, nobody giggled, nobody passed notes or whispered. And while Mr Tiller's up there moving X around, I start to get the feeling that people are looking at me. When I look to my left, all of a sudden Mary Mertins and Rochelle

Quin go back to looking at the board. When I glance to the right, there's Isa Jung and Sommer Hernandez staring at me. They give me nervous little smiles and go back to watching Mr Tiller.

When the passing bell rings, people walk clear around me and act like they're afraid to look at me or something. And when everyone but Marissa's gone, I say to Mr Tiller, "Thanks."

He grins. "It's already been a most interesting day – and it's been my pleasure." He waves an eraser at us. "Go on. Get to class."

So off we run, and the whole way to history Marissa's saying, "I can't believe it! I just can't believe it!"

At lunchtime, I give the blow-by-blow about Heather's little meltdown twice before I remember to tell about finding Chauncy's books and toasting Mr Bell. Marissa says, "This is unbelievable! The Skeleton Man's behind bars and Heather's safely under sedation somewhere – we should celebrate. What do you think, Sammy? What do you want to do?"

I laugh. "I want to go buy a new pair of shoes!"

She says, "You're kidding!"

"Nope. I was thinking maybe I'd go down to the Thrift Store – see if anything's come in. Anyone want to come?"

Dot asks, "Is that the place you were telling me about with that crazy bag lady?"

I laugh. "That would be the one."

Dot says, "You bet! Let me call my mom!"

So she calls her mom, I call Grams and Marissa leaves a message at her house. And before you know it, school's out and we're catching the downtown SMAT bus to the Thrift Store.

The first thing we see is CeCe, all wrapped up in orange and pink scarves, dangling jewellery, digging through a box of stuff this man's brought in.

Dot whispers, "Is that her?"

"Yup."

"Wow – she's something."

We go over to a table and pretend to check out cracked dinner plates so Dot can check out CeCe a little better. CeCe says to the man, "Look, I'm not in the business of paying money for garbage. Most of the stuff you've got here couldn't line a dodo's nest." She pulls something out of the box. "Look at this – what the devil would you do with this? *Wear* it?"

All of a sudden my heart's bumping like a basketball going downcourt. I grab Marissa's arm and say, "Holy smokes! Look!" because I know darn well what you can do with what CeCe's holding. Put out a fire, for one thing. Wear it on Halloween if you're a Marsh Monster, for another.

Marissa starts doing the McKenze dance. "We gotta get it! We gotta get it!"

Dot and I block her from view and say "*Shh!*" because the last thing you should let Tycoon CeCe know is that you *want* something.

When we get her to settle down, we go back to checking out cracked plates. CeCe tells the man, "I couldn't give you ten bucks for the whole box. This stuff just won't move."

He stands there a minute, thinking, so I step up to him and say, "*I'll* give you ten bucks – for just that sweater."

He holds it up. "For *this?*"

Very gently I take it from him and check the label. Sure enough, it's a Louis d'Trent. I dig a ten-dollar bill from my pocket. "Yeah. Here you go."

He laughs. "Done!"

Well, CeCe's looking like a bee in a pickle jar. "Hey! What do you think you're doing?"

The man shrugs. "These ladies just paid me ten dollars for the sweater. You wouldn't give me ten for the whole box!" He picks up his stuff and says, "I think maybe I'll have a garage sale after all," and walks out the door.

CeCe stands there blinking over the top of her glasses at him. Then she turns to me and says, "What's the big idea?"

Now I just want to get *out* of there. Trouble is, Marissa's so excited about finding the sweater that she says, "I don't believe it! This is so cool! That just saved us four hundred and ninety bucks!"

CeCe's ears perk up like a coyote at a gopher hole. "I don't get it. How's this save you four ninety?"

I tug on Marissa. "Come on. We're gonna miss our bus!"

But she's so excited she keeps right on talking, "That sweater's a Louis d'Trent! My mom had one just like it, and Sammy used it to put out a fire. You don't understand – this is going to keep me from being grounded for a year!"

I yank on her and say through my teeth, "Let's get out of here!"

CeCe comes swooping down on us from behind her cash register. "Don't you walk out of here with that! Don't think for a minute you can come into my establishment, put a monkey wrench in a deal I'm making, and then walk off with a five-hundred-dollar sweater! I was going to buy that box from him – I was just making the deal!" She reaches over, pulls ten dollars out of her cash register, and says, "Here! Take this. That sweater is mine. Come on now, take it!"

By now Marissa's got the picture, and let me tell you, we're backing away as fast as we can. And when

CeCe says, "Stop right there or I'll call the police!" we turn around and *run*.

And we keep *on* running until we're safe and sound on the SMAT bus. After we catch our breath, Dot laughs and says, "You don't think she's really going to call the police, do you?"

"CeCe? Nah." Then I laugh and say, "If you really want someone to call the police on us, we could go to Heather's house and ask for the monitor back."

We all bust up, and finally Dot squeaks out, "No, that's OK! She can *have* it!"

We get off the bus at the mall, and we're all going off in our own directions when Dot hollers from the newspaper stand, "Hey! Sammy, come here. Look! You're all over the front page!"

Eighteen

Dot was right. There I was, on the front page of the *Santa Martina Times*. And somehow I wound up there two nights in a row. The first time I was standing between Officer Borsch and Muscles, looking like I was trying to keep them from killing each other. The headline read COPS CLASH AT COURTHOUSE and gave what Hudson called a "speculative overview" of what Muscles and Officer Borsch were fighting about. The article wasn't too far off, so I guess they were shouting even louder than I thought.

The second picture showed me shaking hands with Muscles in front of Bargain Books, and under the picture was the whole story about Mr Bell and the way he'd robbed Chauncy. That headline read HALLOWEEN HEIST! KID CATCHES COSTUMED CROOK. The article mentioned that Muscles was getting a promotion – to what I don't know. I don't think they'll make him chief of police or anything, but if they give him a new partner he'll definitely be celebrating.

A few days after I was on the front page I decided to go over to Hudson's. I found him up on a ladder scraping leaves out of his gutter. He sees me and comes down a few rungs. "Say, young lady, I'm glad you stopped by. Chauncy wants you pay him a visit." He comes down the rest of the way. "Why don't you go over there now?"

Well, it's not like Hudson to try to get rid of me, so I say, "Why?" Then I remember that the last time Chauncy talked to Hudson was years ago. "You talked to him! When did you talk to him?"

Hudson grins and says, "The most recent visit was less than an hour ago."

"The most *recent* visit?" I put my hands on my hips. "All right, tell me everything. How is he?"

He gives me a buttoned little smile and says, "Why don't you go over and ask him yourself?"

I roll my eyes and say, "Hudson!" but I know it's hopeless.

So I head over to Chauncy's, and I'm about to pound on the door when I realize that something's different. The door still looks like a medieval instrument of torture, but through it I can hear music. The kind Grams listens to late at night when she thinks I'm asleep. The kind where violins answer cellos, where horns shout and oboes whisper. The kind where if you close your eyes and wait, you can feel clouds and rain and sunshine.

Chauncy's got electricity! And when I realize that, well, my eyes start watering and my nose starts sniffing, and pretty soon I'm standing there in the middle of a bunch of twigs, crying.

And when I finally quit watering twigs, I take a deep breath, reach up, and ring the doorbell. And who answers? Mrs. D.W. LeBard.

She says, "Samantha! Oh, Chauncy will be so happy to see you!"

I mumble a hello and she lets me in, saying, "Follow me."

The Bush House might have looked the same on the outside, but inside it was really different. And it's not that there was new furniture or anything; it's just that the curtains were open, and with all that light you could see that there were definitely no vampires in Vampire Heaven.

Anyhow, I followed Chauncy's sister-in-law to the back window and we watched Chauncy and Douglas pointing and passing the binoculars back and forth. After a minute Mrs LeBard says, "It almost destroyed all three of them."

"What did?"

"The smoking. And the blame. But look at them now. They're talking again." She takes a deep breath. "I can't thank you enough."

I'm about to tell her that all I did was stick my nose where it wasn't supposed to go, when Chauncy notices me and waves me outside.

As I'm walking out there, I see something I never really thought I'd see – Chauncy LeBard smiling. Really smiling. From ear to ear, from head to toe, he's smiling. And his eyes are twinkling as he buzzes, "Miss Sammy, I am forever in your debt." He motions to his brother, "I know you've met Douglas..."

I grin and say, "You bet."

D.W. grins back. "Please forgive my previous lack of manners. I'm afraid I was being a stubborn old goat."

We all laugh a little, and then Chauncy says, "Good news! Princess's eggs hatched."

"Baby Fuzzballs? Can I see?"

He smiles and hands me the binoculars. Sure enough, there's Fuzzball, busy as a bee, hopping around her nest, pushing who-knows-what down the throats of her chicks. When I get all done looking, I hand the binoculars back to Chauncy and say, "Congratulations!"

Just then Douglas comes back from inside the house and says, "My brother and I have discussed what we could give you as a way of saying thank you for all you've done, and we've decided we'd like you to have this."

He holds out a book. A plum-coloured book with a little frog in the corner. I blink at it a minute and then hand it back. "I can't take this."

Chauncy buzzes, "Please. We *want* you to have it."

I take a deep breath, and for some reason my hands are shaking and I'm feeling kind of weak. I look back and forth between them, and finally I nod and say, "Thank you."

I hang around a little while longer, but when it's time for me to leave I decide to go around the house. I zigzag my way through branches and thorns, and when I get to the sidewalk I turn around and look back for a minute. Then I see the FOR SALE sign next door and it hits me that I'm holding a book that could practically buy Grams and me a house. I turn the book over, and over again, and I realize that there's no way in the world I'm going to sell this book. No way.

I decide that maybe I'll head back to Hudson's. Hudson'll understand. He'll bring out some tea, and we'll sit there on the porch and talk about Chauncy and Douglas and books and life.

And when we're done talking, I'll walk home and tell everything to Grams. And when she gets done deciding that the first thing we should do in the morning is put the book in a safe-deposit box, well, I'm going to do something I don't think you're supposed to do with a rare and valuable book – I'm going to *read* it.

Sammy Keyes

and the **Hotel Thief**

It's not like I was trying to get into trouble. And it's not like it was *my* fault I was stuck inside the apartment. If it was anybody's fault it was Mrs Graybill's. Mrs Graybill lives down the hall and has to be the nosiest person who ever lived. I swear she's got nothing better to do than to stand by her door, waiting for someone to do something she doesn't think they're supposed to be doing. Grams says she's just a bitter old woman, but when I ask *why* she's bitter, Grams doesn't seem to have much of an answer. She usually just shrugs and says, "It happens to people sometimes," and then changes the subject.

Anyhow, it's on account of Mrs Graybill that I was stuck inside when I wanted to be outside. And since there's not much for me to do because everything I own has to be able to fit inside Grams' bottom drawer, I was using the binoculars to at least see what was going on outside.

First I checked out the Pup Parlour. You can see some pretty weird-looking dogs leaving the Pup Parlour. Most of them come out all puffed up and wearing ribbons like they're going to a party instead of home to sleep on the couch. But since we're on the fifth floor and the Pup Parlour's clear down the street, there isn't really much to see if nobody's going in to pick up their puffy dogs. And since nobody *was* going in to pick up their puffy dogs, I didn't spend much time watching.

I didn't waste time at Bargain Books, either. The only interesting thing I ever saw there was when the owner, Mr Bell, chased this kid all the way down to Main Street, yelling at the top of his lungs, "Stop! You come back here and get your filthy bubble gum off my wall!" His face was all red and I thought he was going to have a heart attack. He caught the guy in the middle of the intersection at Broadway and Main and dragged him clear back up to the bookstore by his collar. Then he made him pull the gum off the wall and throw it in a trash can. The boy looked really embarrassed, kind of checking around to see if anyone was watching him pick these big strands of goopy gum off the wall. I waved, but he didn't see me, and pretty soon Mr Bell let him go.

Anyhow, I cruised right by the bookstore and started checking out the hotel. Grams hates the Heavenly Hotel – calls it seedy, but I think she's wrong. One time I even went inside. There was a man with greased-back hair sitting behind the counter reading a newspaper and smoking a cigar. He kind of eyed me from behind the paper, then rolled his cigar over to one side of his mouth and said, "Lookin' for someone?"

I just smiled and shook my head and sat down in one of the fuzzy green chairs they have waiting for you in the lobby. I'd always wanted to sit in a chair like that. The kind with the curvy legs that have paws on the ends of them and then backs that go way up. The backs on the ones in the Heavenly Hotel are pointy – like the pope's hat, only green.

Anyhow, I'm busy trying out one of the chairs when the guy behind the counter says, "You sure?"

I nod and ask him, "How old do you have to be to live here?"

He squints at me and rolls his cigar from one side of his mouth to the other. "Where's your mother?"

Now there's no way I wanted to get into *that*, so I just hopped out of the chair and headed for the door. I'd seen about enough of the Heavenly Hotel anyways. It wasn't anything like Grams had told me. I was expecting a bunch of people hanging around like they do in front of the Salvation Army but all I got to see was some old guy gnawing on a cigar.

Anyhow, from our window you can't see the pope-hat chairs or the guy with the cigar – not even with binoculars. Actually, you can't see much of anything until you're looking at about the third floor. Then things start getting pretty good. Usually you just see people looking out their windows, pointing to stuff on the street or talking on the phone, but sometimes you can see people yelling at each other, which is really strange because you can't *hear* anything.

So I'd started looking at the hotel windows and was checking out the fourth floor when I noticed this guy moving around one of the rooms kind of fast. He disappeared for a little while but when he came back by the window I could see him digging through a handbag like a dog after a gopher. And not only was he pawing through a handbag, he was wearing gloves. Black gloves.

What I should've done was put those binoculars down and call 911. What I did instead was try to get the focus tight on my right eye. When I got the binoculars adjusted so that I could practically see him breathing in and out, I got the strangest feeling that I'd seen this guy before. Either that, or I knew his brother or something.

And I'm trying to get a better look at his face through all his bushy brown hair and beard, when he stuffs a wad of money from the bag into his jacket pocket and then looks up. Right at me.

For a second there I don't think he believed his eyes. He kind of leaned into the window and stared, and I stared right back through the binoculars. Then I did something really, really stupid. I waved.